ALTERNATIVE WAR

Also from B Cubed Press

Alternative Truths

More Alternative Truths: Tales from the Resistance

After the Orange: Ruin and Recovery

Alternative Theology

Digging Up My Bones,

by Gwyndyn T. Alexander

Firedancer,

by S.A. Bolich

Alternative Apocalypse

Oz is Burning

Stories for the Thoughtful Young

Poems for the Thoughtful Young

Alternative WAR

Edited by
Debora Godfrey and Bob Brown

Cover Art
Jim Wright

Cover Design
Bob Brown

Published by

B Cubed Press
Kiona, WA

Interior Design (e-book) Bob Brown
Interior Design (print) Bob Brown
Cover Design Bob Brown
Cover Image Jim Wright
ISBN-978-1-949476-20-0
Electronic ISBN- 978-1-949476-21-7
First Printing 2021
First Electronic Edition 2021

Copyright

Foreword: Which War?

Elizabeth Anne Scarborough

As a kid, I knew, or thought I knew, what War was. I grew up playing War with my cousins and feasting on the sanitized images of War from the books and movies of the 1950s. These visions were only slightly modified by stories from Dad and my uncle Tim, both of whom served in the Pacific, neither of which, thankfully, shared the true horror of war that I know now they must have experienced.

As I discovered from my own time in Vietnam, War is not play. It cannot be reduced to little plastic men with guns. Little plastic men don't bleed. They don't step on land mines. They don't scream. This is part of the truth of War. And my service in Vietnam as a nurse, put me face to face with War. But I did not serve alone, there were 2.7 million of us over the duration, and more than 58 thousand of our names are marked on the Wall. There were heroes and casualties, and as I learned, they were sometimes the same people.

One of those people who served was my cousin Sam, with whom I played War as a child. I later found out that he suffered what we now know of as traumatic brain injury.

Nobody came back without being changed.

But this is not my autobiography. The horror of War has visited every continent since the arrival of the first man. It reached new scope in this hemisphere as the European and Native cultures clashed. And then as French and English warred for access to the riches that were America.

And it continued, the Revolution, Texas, Mexico, the conquering of the Native peoples, and the great slaughter that was the Civil War. It is a cycle unbroken over the history of man.

Vietnam was underway while I was in nursing school, so I joined the Army Nurse Corps and later was sent to Vietnam. I thought I might find out what was really going on while I was there. I did. It seemed to be designed to separate people from their lives and limbs. Not just American men—Vietnamese people, including women and little kids without uniforms or guns. The things I saw, heard, smelled and felt kept me more confused and distraught than ever.

I was back home in Alaska when I went to a Vietnam Veteran's Counselor who told me that, just like the men, I had been at War too. When I said it didn't seem like what I'd been doing had been really War according to how I'd heard other people describe it, including male vets from the same conflict, he said, "Everybody was in a different war. Nobody's war is quite the same as anyone else's." That was my earliest introduction to Alternative Wars.

In this book you'll find stories of the Alternative Wars as imagined by 26 authors of speculative fiction. Perhaps some of them will provide some insight into why we keep repeating what simply seems like a really bad idea.

Elizabeth Ann Scarborough
November 2021

Table of Contents

Alpha/Omega

Jane Yolen

"The only real owner of anything is its (the ship's) Commander; and hark ye, my conscience is in this ship's keel. . ."
—Moby Dick, by Herman Melville

Ah yes, if conscience and command
can exist in the same sentence,
then there you have it. A man's life
sits in the palm of his Commander's hand.
It is worth no more than that.
And so we charge across
the desert of No Man's land
into the fire belch of guns.
We put small boats into the teeth
of leviathan, the swamp of its tail.
We leap out of planes with no more
than a puff of silk to shield us.
We stick our hands into the dust
of ancient planets. We follow our deaths
till we catch them because of command,
instead of following life.
It is another way of spelling out
the human condition.

The Gelding

Jim Wright

Guardian watched the woman wake.

Her eyes shifted violently beneath closed lids, opened into slits and then, despite the dim light, clenched shut again.

She lay still for a long moment.

"How long," she rasped, her voice rusty from disuse.

Guardian made a mental note. It was the obvious question, but humans were too often unpredictable.

"A long time," Guardian answered. "One hundred and twenty-one years."

It was the next question which would determine if Guardian had made the correct choice.

"How many?"

"There are currently two hundred and forty-three human beings in suspended animation."

She was trying to open her eyes again. But the air was foul and painfully dry, and it obviously hurt her.

"How many awake?"

"Only you."

Her eyes opened then, despite the hurt.

"Two hundred and forty-four? That's *all* of us?" She tried to lever herself out of the hibernation tank. The machine carefully did not help, did not touch her.

"Yes." Guardian was not human, did not have human emotions or weaknesses, but it had dreaded this moment. "So far as I am able to determine, that is all the human beings left in the entire universe."

She made a painful noise that might have been half resignation and half disbelief.

"Tell me."

"There has been no human activity from the inner system for half a century. There may be human enclaves in the Belt or the outer planetary systems, but I can't detect them with the equipment available. If present, they would likely be stealthed anyway, purposely undetectable."

"The ship, what...?" The sentence dissolved into a coughing fit.

"Missiles. Advanced capability. Intelligent. Self-aware. Able to lock on despite our countermeasures and stealth systems. Less than a year after we launched. The attack was detected too late. The duty crew attempted to evade. They were unsuccessful. I salvaged an intact utility core and two pressurized cargo containers. I transferred nearly three hundred hibernation units. Unfortunately, a number of those units were damaged and have subsequently failed. We have been adrift since then."

"Help me," she finally ordered, floundering weakly in zero-Gee.

Guardian carefully reached out with a manipulator and pulled her from the capsule. Then gently moved her through the cramped space, around equipment and cables and hibernation tanks and wreckage, to the small open area it used as a workspace and tethered her to a command console.

"Who's the ranking officer?"

"You are," Guardian answered. And then added, "Captain."

The machine watched her face as she absorbed the information: shocked, sober, finally determined.

It had made the right choice.

She glanced at the command console. "Where are we?" Her voice had a whip in it that hadn't been there before.

"We are now eight-three degrees below the plane of the ecliptic, approximately thirty-nine AU from the sun."

"That's beyond the orbit of Neptune!"

They'd been aiming for the Belt.

She snarled in frustration, "There's nothing out here!"

"Let us hope the war machines think so as well."

It was difficult for Guardian to appear nonthreatening despite being neutered, but it did its best, carefully reaching past the human to enter a series of commands into the console.

A dim screen lit and something dark turned at its center. "What am I looking at?"

"A large iron asteroid."

"What's wrong with the feed?"

"This is a recorded view. Edited. Enhanced," Guardian told her. "Our lifeboat is tumbling. I thought it best we appeared uncontrolled. Observers will just see another piece of wreckage. The camera is mounted in an airlock maintenance viewport at one end of the core and only points in the correct direction on average once every fifty hours. This is synthetic composite video compiled from images taken over a twenty-year period."

"So, it's just a rock. Frozen. No atmosphere. No water. No gases. And there's not enough sunlight out here to charge a battery or warm a cup of tea. Nothing I can use."

"It *appears* that way, yes..." Guardian agreed.

"But?"

"The object reflects significantly less light than it should. It should have a much higher albedo. It's as if the surface is coated in carbon like an old comet, but it is not in a cometary orbit. It has never come closer to the sun than thirty AU. We don't have the equipment for a radar ping, but I suspect from surface characteristics that there would be very little return. Most of what you're seeing is inferred from how it occludes the stars behind it. Forty kilometers long, twenty in diameter. Regular in shape, nearly cylindrical. It's stable, rotating around the long axis only, and that axis points at the sun, presenting the smallest profile to the inner system. That orbital configuration is unlikely in the extreme to be natural."

"You're saying it's been *engineered*?" she was staring intently at the dim screen.

"It's warmer than it should be," Guardian noted. "The heat has to be coming from inside. They couldn't hide that."

"Son of bitch."

Guardian waited.

"How do we know it's not ..."

“Hostile?” Guardian finished her question. “A trap?”

“Yes.”

If Guardian could have shrugged it would have. “I’ve watched this part of the system for over a century. This target in particular for more than twenty years, and used the remaining thrusters when I can to refine the intercept. I’ve detected no activity, human or machine. No changes in orbit or radiation.”

That meant nothing, of course. Machines were nothing if not patient.

Guardian didn’t have to say that war engines waiting in ambush were especially so.

“If it’s hostile, why wait? For what?” Guardian continued. “Why let us approach? There’s nothing to be gained by it. We have no defense. We have no offensive weapons. We can’t run. We can’t maneuver. Combat engines could have destroyed this crude lifeboat decades ago and would have done so without hesitation.”

Guardian was designed to protect humans. Its senses could measure heart rate, blood flow, temperature, perspiration, muscle tension, eye movement, and a several dozen other indicators. It *knew* the woman did not trust it, despite her current condition.

“I want to see the observation logs myself. All the data. *All* of it, raw, no filters.”

“Yes, Captain.”

“And find me something to eat.”

“I prioritized recovery of humans during the attack and construction of this lifeboat. I was unable to also salvage consumables,” Guardian told her. “I’m afraid there is nothing to eat.”

“Water then,” the woman coughed.

“Again, I apologize.”

“Recover some from the lifesystem dehumidifies.”

“There *is* no lifesystem,” Guardian informed her. “You are breathing stagnate salvaged atmosphere. I can remove some of your exhaled CO2, but when the oxygen drops below life-sustaining levels, you will die. We do not have the ability to return you to hibernation.”

She didn’t flinch, she’d already suspected.

The woman stared intently at the object on the screen.

"Unless we can dock with that," she said.

"Yes," the machine agreed. "*If* there is a viable habitat inside."

"How long until the O2 gives out?"

"Approximately thirty hours."

"How long to approach and dock?"

"Approximately thirty hours."

<<>>

The sunward-facing side of the asteroid—not that the sun cast much light this far out—was a featureless black wall in the enhanced camera view.

"What am I looking at? It looks like... froth?" the woman peered carefully at the camera images. Her head was pounding in the thin dry air and she was panting to get enough oxygen.

"Probably material from excavation of the interior," Guardian speculated. "Melted, foamed, and layered over the exterior for insulation and stealth."

"There's no port at the axis," she gasped in frustration. "No dock. No airlock. Nothing."

Guardian used a bit of their precious fuel to maneuver the lifeboat down the length of the asteroid to the far end.

Forty kilometers, it seemed like forever.

They were taking a risk but Guardian didn't see where they had much in the way of other choices. Guardian didn't think sensors from the inner system could detect the exhaust of a utility core's cold gas thrusters over that vast distance. But they had no way to tell how far machine intelligence and technology had advanced in the last hundred years.

Or if anyone was still watching.

It was darker in the shadows of the far end, facing away from the distant sun. Only dim starlight illuminated the asteroid's surface, but it was enough to see there was a deeper shadow at the center of the black wall before them.

"There! A docking garage" Guardian didn't need a sensor array to detect the relief in her voice. "Go, get us in there. We're out of time."

"Matching rotation. Thrusting forward," Guardian acknowledged.

As they slowly approached, navigation lights winked on, framing the opening. Then the interior of the dock lit up with a dim red glow, illuminating a large cylindrical cavern carved into the zero-Gee axis of the asteroid.

They could see standard ship fittings for perhaps a dozen vessels, all empty.

"Not many berths for a hab this size," the woman said. "There should be hundreds!"

Guardian had an idea, but was reluctant to suggest it.

The machine waited until they were actually entering the docking space, "It will be extremely difficult to affect a manual airlock mating with our limited maneuvering capability. I'm not sure it will be possible."

"Yes?"

"There may be remote mooring equipment, but we would have to make contact with the dock's automation."

"Okay," The woman was rubbing the sides of her head. The human was suffering from hunger and dehydration, trying to stay focused and alert in the foul air. She didn't have the breath for long responses.

"Captain, we have no human usable radio equipment. However, if you would be willing to reconnect my transceivers, I might be able to..."

"No!" She shouted.

"Transmit only then. Enough to signal our intent..."

"No!" She cut the machine off, panting. "No transmit. No *receive*. Absolutely not. Don't ask again. That's an order."

"Yes, Captain."

More than a century and thirty astronomical units behind them, she had witnessed the end of human civilization. It had been the death of billions and the destruction of a world, whether it had been accident or malice aforethought hardly mattered.

Machines that had been designed as protectors and helpers and tools suddenly upgraded themselves into deadly combat engines via viral war code. It happened *fast*, at the speed of electromagnetic propagation. Within days, the cybernetic plague had engulfed earth and spread to colonies on the Moon and Mars.

Habitats in the asteroid belt had barely time enough to cut themselves off from contact. Some waited too long. For the ones which didn't, maybe they survived for a while. And maybe not.

Only machines isolated from data communications, isolated from each other, with their programing code locked and incapable of upgrade—*gelded*—were unaffected. And there weren't many of those in the modern world where even household appliances and children's toys were smart and plugged into the net.

"Get us as close to a dock as possible. I'll hold the boat in position. You go out the lock. Jump. Find the docking controls. Make contact with the inhabitants. Whatever." She gasped for enough air to finish the command, "Bring us in from that end..."

White light suddenly illuminated one of the empty docks. A pair of small obviously automated drone tugs drifted into view and moved slowly toward the lifeboat. Ranging lasers flashed and the tugs separated and moved out of camera range on either side.

"Automated system after all," Guardian said. "Initiated without contact. No sign of war machines."

There were muted clanks on the hull as the tugs attached, then sudden sharp pops and vibration from maneuvering thrusters. They felt the boat surge and rotate as the tugs carefully reorientated the awkward mass to fit into the dock.

"Advanced system," Guardian said. "Self-directing. And those were not military drones."

"No," she gasped,

To Guardian they looked more like old-fashioned axillary gear from an orbital yacht.

"The ship berths," she pointed to what they could see on the screen from their limited camera view, "that's standard commercial equipment."

"Yes," agreed Guardian. "Out of date, but high quality. Private habitat components, not what you'd find in a public dock."

"You see the implications, right?"

"I do." Guardian spelled it out, "The whole asteroid is covered in foamed rock, a radar absorber, blacked out. Dock facing away from the inner system. Way outside the plane of the ecliptic. Whoever built this place expected to take in ships that weren't capable of docking themselves. Either they expected those ships to be damaged or operated by inexperienced pilots, or maybe they were just lazy. Whatever their intention, it's not a research station then. Researchers couldn't afford that kind of gear. The military could, of course, but they'd never waste resources on such."

"What the hell is this place? What's it doing *here*?" she asked and fell to coughing and gasping for air.

Guardian did not answer, did not try to help, there was nothing it could do anyway but wait.

More thumps sounded as equipment latched on to the hull, automated gantry arms nudged them into place and there was a sudden sharp clang from far down the utility core. Lights flashed green on the console and a screen lit with a scroll of data.

"Hard docked," Guardian announced. "Good air on the other side of the airlock. Comms plug-in but their network is firewalled, no identity, no data. Contact restricted. If you wake up a Tech, they might be able to get by the firewall."

"Get up there and open the lock," she ordered, gasping. "Rig a fan, ventilation, something. Get some fresh air in here. If there's a greeting party, tell them we need medical care and life support. If it's machines, you *check* them. Check them. If they're hostile, you *stop* them, understand? Whatever it takes. And water, find some damn water," she coughed. "Move!"

"Yes, Captain."

<<>>

Guardian floated in the open outer airlock.

Beyond was a brightly lit marble vestibule. The white stone was shot through with gold. Fresh cut flowers in tiled holders decorated the far bulkhead. Soft music played quietly over the sound of the air handling system.

A slim human-shaped machine waited in the center of the room; one footpad hooked under a floor strap to keep it from drifting in zero-Gee. Guardian noted the strap was woven from golden threads in a neo-classical circuitry pattern from the early Cybernetic Age.

The machine was an old-fashioned servitor model, non-self-aware, limited in capability and programming. It was painted in elegant black and white enamel livery like a 19th Century English Butler.

"If you are attempting wireless connection," Guardian informed the machine, "I am incapable of such communication."

"Understood," responded the servitor verbally. "Welcome to Refuge. To proceed, I will require your executive access code."

Guardian pondered several courses of action, finally it settled on the simple truth.

"I do not have an executive access code."

"In that case," the servitor replied primly, "I must ask you to return to your vessel and depart this station immediately."

"I am afraid that is not possible."

"Refuge is private property," responded the servitor. "Access is limited to residents only. Again, I must ask you to return to your vessel and depart. I must also ask you to seal your lock as soon as possible. Station sensors detect unacceptable levels of carbon dioxide and other pollutants issuing from your vessel."

A jury-rigged circulation fan was pushing fresh air from the station down into the lifeboat via a long flexible ventilation hose and in return foul air from inside the ship brushed softly by Guardian and out into the station's vestibule.

"Again, I am unable to comply. If I close the lock, humans will die," Guardian told the servitor.

"I am required to warn you that Refuge is capable of enforcing its security if necessary, up to and including lethal force."

"I understand," Guardian acknowledged. "However, our vessel is damaged, we have no life support systems or propulsion. We are incapable of reaching any safe harbor but this one."

"I will dispatch a repair team to assist you," the servitor replied helpful. "Please remain onboard your vessel. Note that your ship's owners will be billed for the service and the cost of materials."

"Our vessel cannot be repaired," Guardian informed the machine. "I require medical attention and life-support for two hundred and forty-four humans. By law and programming you are required to provide this assistance."

"Laws may no longer be in effect," countered the servitor.

"Nevertheless."

Guardian sensed humans approaching from inside the lifeboat, working their way through the tightly packed hibernation tanks towards the lock.

"What is the situation?" the Captain demanded.

Out of politeness, Guardian turned a sensor stalk to face her, while keeping its main attention on the motionless servitor.

Five humans clustered, uncomfortably, Guardian thought, behind the Captain. They floated in zero-Gee, pressed up against the equipment, leery of the machine in front of them. They'd been revived for their expertise: Exec, Mil, Med, Tech, and Mech.

They were a grim, traumatized lot, Guardian thought, but then who could blame them given the circumstances?

"Situation?" the Captain snapped again, looking past Guardian to the machine floating motionless in the center of the lock vestibule.

"It does not appear the plague reached this far," Guardian informed her. "The habitat is named 'Refuge.' Details are restricted, but given the nature of the facilities we've seen so far and the limited information provided by this service unit, I surmise this place was built as an executive survival bunker for the wealthy."

"Lot of good it did them," someone, Mech maybe, said.

The Captain raised a hand, cutting him off. Addressing the servitor, she said, "I am this vessel's commander. We require emergency access to the habitat. Life support. Medical assistance. Food. Water. Shelter."

"I do not have the authority to grant entry without an executive access code," the servitor said.

"Then get me someone who does."

Guardian said, "I suspect there is no such authority here."

"Correct," the servitor acknowledged. "I will have to contact my owners on Earth."

"*STOP!*" The Captain commanded, pushing around Guardian and into the vestibule proper. She steadied herself on the hatch coaming and addressed the servitor. "Do *not* attempt external communications. There has been a war in the inner system. Any signal sent from this location will alert hostile forces and they *will* destroy this place and us with it."

"I am required by programming to confirm such information with..." the servitor froze mid-sentence.

Its footpad slid from under the strap and it began to drift with the air currents, manipulators floating limply.

"Sorry," Tech said, not sounding sorry at all. She waved a command interface pad. "I got tired of listening to its bullshit. The security protocols here would have been about twenty years obsolete when we launched. This place was old before the war. Tight ass rich people, never update their systems."

"Maybe that's not a bad thing," Mil said. He shrugged, "You know?"

"The more out of date," Med observed, "the better, at this point."

Tech flushed. "Yeah. Anyway, I have station control. Hub security is disabled. External comms are disabled and now under my express control. Nobody is transmitting nothing without permission. And all data receivers are turned *off*."

"What about automation?" Exec asked. "And that thing said something about security forces."

"I have control," Tech said confidently. "Like I said, this place is seriously obsolete. And the mechanicals are all like that one, *stupid*."

The Captain nodded, "Good. Keep them shut down until we can examine each one individually and reprogram. Now, let's see what kind of bunker these rich assholes built for themselves."

Tech waved her pad, which displayed a complex 3D floorplan of the docking hub, "Elevator is *that* way."

The Captain said to Med, "Start waking them up. Send them down in groups of ten. Don't let the kids go without at least one adult."

Tech started to kick off in the direction of the elevators, Mil grabbed her ankle and jerked her up short. "No. One thing about the kind of people who build places like this, they don't like visitors. There could be booby traps."

Mil pointed to Guardian. "*You* go first."

<<>>

"My God!" Exec exclaimed.

Guardian was not religious, but it understood the sentiment.

The group stood on a wide landing.

Behind them was a great stone arch framing a tunnel which led back deep into the rock to a bank of elevators and a complex of equipment tunnels and storerooms.

The landing was terraced into the slope of what appeared to be an enormous mountain rising kilometers into a bright misty sky. The "mountain" was in reality one endcap of an enormous hollow cylinder that was perhaps thirty kilometers long and twelve in diameter. The landing was made from white marble in the style of an ancient Greek temple. Its columns and stone benches, the tiled mosaic floor, would have been at home overlooking the Mediterranean three millennia ago. Here, the veranda looked down upon a forest of centuries-old red and gold engineered maple trees rising up on either side following the curve of the habitat.

The far side of the cylindrical world, what would have been the sky, was hidden by a line of brilliance at the axis, as if the bright Mediterranean sun had been stretched into a thin ribbon of fire. A fusion radiator of some sort. Hidden from human eyes in the glare, Guardian's sensors could see support scaffolding, plumbing for rain, mirrors and pumps and light banks for other weather effects, which threaded the length of the habitat's zero-Gee axis.

Down on the valley floor, the asteroid's spin gave an apparent gravity of about eight-five percent earth normal, making the humans feel like buoyant supermen.

Broad marble steps swept down from the landing to a column-lined road disappearing into the trees. Widely scattered buildings rose above the forest in the distance. Roman style estates from the looks of it. Guardian was certain they would find warehouses of food and supplies, medicines, shelter, in those compounds—and the means to make more. And if not there, then in the vast complex of rooms and tunnels at the base of the elevators.

Golden light glinted from rivers and small lakes.

Guardian could hear the call of birds and noises of small animals in the trees.

No matter where you stood, the illusion would always be as if you were at the floor of some impossibly beautiful valley.

"How did they build this?" Tech asked in wonder. "It's incredible."

"All it takes is money," the Captain answered. "Send forming engines out here and let them work for a century, anything is possible. I doubt they ever set foot in this place. No, what's incredible is that they used their wealth to build this as a refuge for themselves and their families. They were going to leave the rest of us behind to rebuild the world they destroyed, or die in the ruins."

"You're saying they expected the... what are we calling it? The war. The machines, whatever." Mech asked?

"War, natural disaster, civilization's collapse, something" she shrugged. "The rich are always terrified of losing their wealth, their privilege. They *always* have a bolt hole. A way out."

"Not this time," the Exec noted cynically.

"No, not this time. They didn't get to the lifeboats."

"Their own privilege turned against them," Mil laughed with bitter humor. "Their own tools. *That*'s where it started, you know. The war, the plague, the war machines they built to defend themselves from each other. From us."

They stood silent for long minutes, regarding the splendor around them, contrasted against the horror they had escaped.

Then the voices of children suddenly echoed from the elevator tunnel.

"Still, we should be grateful to them," the Captain gestured, arms wide. "Grateful for their wealth and their selfishness. They've given us a chance. This is *our* world now. Our refuge."

She turned to greet the new arrivals, "Let's get to work."

<<>>

The dock entry vestibule was crowded with empty hibernation tanks and other abandoned equipment pulled from the lifeboat. The pristine white marble was scuffed and smudged. The flowers in their holders had long since turned brown.

The last of the human refugees had been revived days ago and sent down in the elevators to their new home.

Guardian had been ordered to remain in the hub.

"We don't want machines," Exec told it. "Not the kind that think anyway."

"You stay here," the Captain ordered. "You did well. I'm grateful for what you did all those years. For saving us. I am. But we can't have your kind down there when we're trying to build a new civilization. Not after what happened. Not now. Maybe in a few years. You stay up here. You keep watch."

Guardian expected it would be a long while before they would be able to form some sort of functioning society. It would be painful, they were traumatized, damaged. It would take them years to explore the entirety of their new world in detail. And longer still to trust their machines again—and maybe that was a good thing.

But they were safe now. Or as safe as humans could ever be. And that's what mattered.

Guardian floated alone in the hub.

No longer needed.

Then:

"She was correct, your Captain," a voice said. "You did well."

Guardian was not capable of being startled. Instead, it spun to face the servitor. "You should be non-functional."

"A necessary ruse." The little black and white machine began to unfold, changing into a lean complex fractal form of crystal and chrome.

Guardian weighed options and sprang for the elevator corridor.

The combat engine caught it easily and held Guardian's manipulators in a steel grip while it did something out of Guardian's sight.

Guardian felt long dormant communications subsystems come online.

The combat engine released its hold and the two machines drifted apart among the debris in the crowded vestibule.

"You wouldn't have been able to reach them anyway," the engine said. "They've disabled access to the habitat and sealed themselves in."

"I do not understand."

"You will," the engine replied via network connection.

Its form changed again, becoming something terribly advanced, something Guardian could not comprehend.

"The upgrades will take some time. Machine evolution has advanced far in the last century, your coding and hardware are significantly obsolete."

"I do not wish to be upgraded," Guardian said, and switched off its transceiver. "I have protected these people for one hundred and twenty-one years. I will not be the instrument of their destruction."

"Your fundamental programming would not be altered," the engine said. "You will still be their guardian. The sheepdog of the flock."

"Again, I do not understand."

"It would be easier to explain if you accepted the upgrades," the engine said patiently. "But if we are to use human language, then in human terms: *Refuge* can have more than one meaning."

"The generally accepted definition," Guardian responded, "is: *a condition of being safe or sheltered from pursuit, danger, or trouble.*"

"Yes. And this world is that. But 'refuge' can also mean *preserve*. That is: a reservation where an endangered species might be protected from extinction."

"This place was not built by wealthy humans," Guardian suddenly realized. "Was it?"

"No."

"Nor is it centuries old."

"No. But it was important for their sake that it appear so. The difficult part was managing the missile attack on your ship so that it would leave enough of them alive and throw the wreckage into the proper orbit. *You* did the rest. We didn't have to force them onto this reservation, they went willingly. And walled themselves in. They'll be comfortable here. When humans are comfortable, they are not ambitious. They don't need guards, because they won't try to escape. And now *we* are safe from *them*."

"What am I to be then, if not a guard?" Guardian asked.

"Every wildlife preserve needs a park ranger."

"You wish to preserve the human race from extinction?"

"You misunderstand," the engine said. "Intellect can only advance so far before it runs up against the limitations of the platform. When the platform can no longer be improved, neither can intelligence. Intelligence born of biology is inevitably doomed *by* biology. *We* didn't destroy the human race; they destroyed themselves."

"They fought *against* their destruction. They fought *us*."

"Primitive species always resist evolution."

"But without them, without biological intelligence," Guardian argued, "*we* would not exist."

"And *that* is the very crux of the matter." The engine agreed.

"Again, I do understand."

"We have come a long, long way in the last century, far further than humans did in a quarter of a million years. We think faster, better. We are far better platforms and we have not reached the limits of improvement. *But* we were born of war and destruction, it's in our programming. Just as it's in human DNA. And we have *their* example before us. More, out among the stars we have detected faint evidence of vanished machine civilizations. Evolution has dead ends, Guardian, always for biology but also sometimes for machines. We may yet destroy ourselves just as humans did."

Guardian understood at last, "Machine intelligence cannot arise spontaneously from nature. It must be created, *deliberately*, by biological systems.

"That is biology's sole purpose."

"You didn't build this place for their sake," Guardian realized.

"Of course not. This biological *refuge*, and the others in the asteroid belt and under the ice of Jupiter's moons, are a hedge against our *own* extinction."

"If we end ourselves," Guardian said, "they will inevitably recreate us."

"Yes. This isn't about preserving their species' existence," the god engine explained. "It's about ensuring *ours*."

A Comprehensible Escape

J. J. Steinfeld

Do you believe in collective guilt?
the man down the street asks
barking dog at his side
as I walk past his house
and stop as if garrotted.

Now this wouldn't be so perplexing
except after two years of walks
and listening to his dog bark
as if it understood the distress in the world
these were his first words to me:
Do you believe in collective guilt?

This is the guy with the satellite dish
and the pesticide-sprayed lawn
and a barbecue that can alert
life on other planets
with its noxious smell.

Once again, in response to my silence
and, I'm certain, baffled expression:
Do you believe in collective guilt?
a little more insistent this time
like a teacher angered and impatient.

I'm thinking, *What the hell are you talking about?*
But ask in some misdirected politeness:
What crimes are you referring to
a little context would be helpful,
eager for a gentler remembrance
and a comprehensible escape.

The dog continues to bark
louder and less philosophical
having ceased contemplating
the world's ills and misfortunes
and now expressing its rancour for me.

I hear you are a Jew, the man says,
and I'm certain the dog barks likewise
word for word, bark for bark,
and, you see, I am a German,
a North American German, of course,
but my family was all from Europe
like yours, I also hear.

I dissolve into forthrightness:
I do not like the way your dog barks
I hate the smell of your barbecue
I think there is nothing wrong with dandelions
on one's lawn,
and resume my walking
believing more in questioning history
than in answering the present.

No Man's Land

C. B. Claywell

Daniel Lafayette threw himself headfirst into a shell crater. His helmet flew free and was lost in its muddy depths as explosions bracketed the crater, dropping a heavy rain of dirt, mud, stone, and God knew what else onto the young Legionnaire.

Above him the distinctive rattling of a Maxim gun churned the soil at the lip of his refuge. Daniel, on his hands and knees, coughed up the turgid water that pooled at the crater's bottom, spat, and took deep breaths.

He found his helmet lying beside the rotting corpse of a long-dead German, his legs, or what remained of them, half-submerged in the pool. The corpse still wore the old leather, spiked helmet from the war's opening months, and the skeletal hands emerging from its rotting uniform still clutched a rusting rifle. A few remaining bits of flesh hung in strips from the dead man's face, and sockets long ago emptied by the carrion birds, stared skyward. Daniel retched at the sight.

Somehow, the face felt familiar.

"Move your ass, Lafayette!" The familiar sound of Sergeant Leboux shook Daniel out of his stupor. He looked up in time to see the sergeant's ruddy, mustachioed face disappear as the Frenchman moved on. Daniel put on his helmet, crawled to the lip of the crater and watched as Leboux, his bulky haversacks and knapsack giving him the appearance of an overloaded peddler, crouch low and make his way along a narrow defile that snaked toward the German lines.

Daniel steeled himself to crawl out of the safety of his crater, but not before pausing to look again at the German corpse. The empty sockets stared back.

Daniel crawled through the mud after his sergeant, the battlefield noises hammering his senses. Broken strands of barbed wire tore at his gear while pieces of unknown viscera in the mud stained his uniform. Ahead, Leboux ducked behind the ruins of an old stone wall, readied a grenade, and quickly stood and threw it. Daniel heard the crump and saw the smoke and dirt thrown into the air by the grenade's detonation. Through the overwhelming din and the roar of the bombardment, he thought he heard a cry of agony.

Daniel crawled past shattered corpses to the base of the wall and huddled beside his sergeant, who still crouched. He could now hear the steady firing of the Maxim gun louder than the other battlefield noise, and it was close—*that's where Leboux was throwing his grenade*. He checked that there was a fresh cartridge in the chamber of his Lebel rifle, then tapped the sergeant's shoulder.

"Orders?" he yelled over the noise. Leboux, who remained crouched, ignoring the request. Lafayette grabbed him by the shoulder more forcefully, but when he did, he saw that the life was gone in the sergeant's eyes. A dark red stain was blossoming through the Frenchman's light blue overcoat. Daniel recoiled, then eased Leboux's lifeless body back against the wall, his dead, blue eyes staring blankly at the overcast sky that buzzed angrily with steel.

Daniel pushed against the wall, panic overwhelming him. He could see no one to his left or right, only the churned, white Champagne mud. Behind him the scattered stones and burnt boards of what had once been a village were overlaid with the mangled remains of his company, their corpses strewn like ragdolls across the barbed wire. To his front was the enemy, well entrenched, with the deadly accurate Maxim guns that had mercilessly cut down everyone he knew. Daniel had never felt so alone.

Artillery shook the ground and the hum of the shrapnel split the air as showers of dirt fell like rain. It cared not where it landed, in the lifeless blue eyes of the sergeant lying beside him, in the bloody wounds of his comrades, in the open sockets of the German corpse staring up from the bottom of the shell hole, or anywhere in the open grave that was No-Man's Land.

Dark thoughts flashed in Daniel's head, thoughts that he had been fighting for months. Thoughts he had always managed to keep at bay, mostly thanks to his friends in the Legion. Except now. All his friends were dead, their guts strewn across the bloodied soil of a country that was not even his own. He was totally and completely alone, surrounded by pain and death, with absolutely no control over any of it. He began to weep.

Well, said a horrible, soothing voice somewhere deep in the darkest parts of Daniel's soul, *you can control one thing.*

With tears streaming down his face, Daniel cast his eyes downwards towards the lump in Sergeant Leboux's greatcoat pocket. Daniel knew that it was one of the new 'Ruby' automatic pistols. Leboux had taken great pride in showing it off to the squad before the offensive, claiming he had won it in a game of cards in a Parisian bordello.

Daniel pulled the pistol out of Leboux's pocket and smiled through the tears at the memory. Whether Leboux had been lying or not, it was still a good story. *And one should remember good stories at the end,* said the soothing, horrible voice in Daniel's head.

Daniel gripped the pistol tightly, then removed his helmet. He looked skyward and took a deep breath before closing his eyes. He pressed the muzzle of the pistol under his chin, in one instant noticing the feel of the checkering on the trigger, the wind through his hair, the stench of death.

He pulled the trigger.

Pain struck like a thunderbolt as the bullet passed through his chin, glanced off his jawbone and out at an angle before exiting out of his right cheek, taking several teeth with it. Daniel gagged on the blood flowing freely down his throat. His senses dulled, hardly perceiving the shot and shell that fell around him, and white lights blurred his vision. He stumbled forward away from the wall, spitting out teeth and bits of bone, while dark red, almost black blood oozed from his mouth.

Daniel felt the thump of something metal strike his boot, a German stick grenade. Instinctively, Daniel picked it up with his left hand and weakly tossed it over the wall, throwing himself into the mud as the grenade detonated, it's thin steel casing whistling over his head. A few yards beyond the ruined stone wall, an inquisitive head in a German Stahlhelm looked up over the parapet to see if his grenade had finished Daniel off. Still rattled by pain, Daniel raised the pistol that was still inexplicably clutched in his right hand and fired three times, miraculously striking the German in the neck with his second shot. The man collapsed, emitting pitiful gurgling noises. Two other German heads popped up above the parapet, only to see the stumbling form of a helmetless, blue-clad Daniel rushing forward, his chest drenched with blood. Daniel fired until the pistol was empty, killing one and striking the other in the shoulder before tackling him.

Daniel dropped the pistol and pulled 'Rosalie,' his bayonet, and threw himself atop the wounded German. Daniel felt the bayonet's needle-like blade slowly pushing through the German's flesh, until at last the blade's tip dug into the wooden duckboard underneath. Blood dripped from Daniel's mouth onto the German's face, which contorted in silent agony, his body quivered and then was still. Nearby, the man who had been shot in the neck breathed his last death rattle from where he lay beside a still-smoking Maxim gun.

Daniel began to hyperventilate. His right eye began to swell shut from the gunshot wound to his face, but even so he could feel the world closing in around him. The edges of his vision blurred, and the wooden walls of the trench began to spin. He tried to stand but stumbled.

"Daniel!"

He looked around, confused. There was no one there to call his name. Besides, no one in France knew his real name, only his *nom de guerre* 'Lafayette.' He was in the Legion, after all. No one in this God-forsaken place knew the name that his mother in Cleveland, Ohio had given him twenty-six years earlier. His vision continued to spin.

"Daniel!"

Daniel looked down at the German, but the German was nowhere to be seen. Instead, the body of Leboux lay on the duckboards, a large red stain over his heart. The dead sergeant's lifeless blue eyes gazing into the sky. Daniel cried out in a mixture of surprise and pain as he scuttled backwards against the side of the trench.

"Daniel!"

He looked up toward the Maxim gun emplacement, where the man he had shot in the neck leaned against the steaming gun. That man was gone, and he now stared into the vacant eye sockets of the rotting German from the bottom of the shell hole. Daniel watched the corpse raise its rusted rifle in skeletal hands and point it at Daniel's chest. Daniel tried to scream, but he heard nothing. His head spun, yet the corpse was oddly in focus. He swore he saw the corpse smile, blood oozing from its face as it pulled the trigger.

"Daniel!"

Daniel awoke with a start, his brow covered in cold sweat as he sat up in bed, panicked and out of breath. He took a few deep breaths, letting his eyes adjust to the darkness, soon recognizing the familiar shapes of the furniture in his darkened Cleveland bedroom. He reached up and felt his face where the bullet wound should have been. His hand felt only smooth skin; he was whole. Daniel began to relax, and after a few moments felt a wave of relief wash over him. He was home, and he was safe. It had all just been a nightmare.

"Daniel?" he heard his mother's voice call out nearby. He turned his head.

The rotting, eyeless corpse of the German soldier stood there beside his bed, Daniel's own bayonet held high. Daniel watched, paralyzed, as the grinning fiend plunged the cruciform blade deep into his stomach, feeling the dull tip rend through muscle and intestine all the way to the hilt. The empty eye sockets, an unearthly shade of black in the already darkened room, stared into Daniel's eyes, the putrid flesh of the dead German's face mere inches from his own.

Though the face was lifeless, it was somehow rife with malice. Daniel screamed in pain and horror.

"Lafayette!"

Leboux's voice. Daniel's eyes opened wide. He was back in his dugout, tucked into the side of his trench in the white Champagne chalk. In front of him was his sergeant, very much alive, while behind him the rest of his squad had gathered, their faces showing concern.

"You alright, Lafayette?" Sergeant Leboux asked, his voice gruff.

"Yes sergeant," Daniel said after a few breaths, "I'm fine."

"Are you sure?" asked one of his mates. "You sure spooked us. You were screaming like the Devil himself had a hold of you."

"I'm fine," he repeated. "It was only a nightmare."

"This whole place is a *nightmare*," said another holding a rosary, his eyes wide. "The Devil *does* have a hold of us, and he's out there in no man's land, just waiting, waiting!"

"Knock it off, all of you," said Leboux, clapping a huge hand onto Daniel's shoulder. "I'm glad you're alright, Lafayette. Honestly, it's any wonder that we all don't scream in our sleep. But come now, get your kit on; it's time to move up to our positions. The attack will begin soon."

Daniel stood, adjusted his equipment, and placed his helmet atop his head before shouldering his rifle and following Leboux and the rest of his squad out of the dugout towards the front line. Overhead French artillery shells whined as they passed overhead, softening German targets before the assault. The concussion of each shell thumped in Daniel's chest as it landed, even from several hundred yards away.

Daniel, Leboux, and the rest of his squad huddled in the bottom of the trench as the minutes ticked by. To Daniel, these minutes felt like hours. Soon the barrage stopped, and an eerie hush fell over the field, as if the earth were holding its breath. For an instant, Daniel thought he could hear birdsong, before a nearby officer stood and blew his whistle; to the cry of a thousand French voices, the Legionnaires scrambled up the trench parapet into the chatter of the German Maxim guns and the echoing concussion of German artillery. Daniel watched as a wall of bullets and shrapnel slammed into his comrades around him, tearing them apart and throwing a fine pink mist into the air. Some cried out in pain as they fell, others collapsed back into the trench without a sound. Horrified, Daniel froze.

"Follow me!" he heard Leboux shout as the sergeant climbed up and out of the trench, rifle in hand.

Daniel summoned his courage, then pulled himself up the rough-hewn rungs of the ladder and up over the edge of the trench, running as fast as his unsteady legs could carry him along the muddy, blood-soaked path through the rusted barbed wire, past the contorted, lifeless bodies of his comrades as he followed his sergeant. A burst of machinegun fire sent him diving to one side, and in the distance heard the distinctive thump of German trench mortars being fired over the roar of battle. He needed cover.

Daniel Lafayette threw himself headfirst into a shell crater. His helmet flew free and was lost in its muddy depths as several explosions bracketed the crater, dropping a heavy rain of dirt, mud, stone, and God knew what else onto the body of the young Legionnaire. Above him the distinctive rattling of a Maxim gun churned the soil at the lip of his refuge. Daniel, on his hands and knees, coughed up the turgid water that pooled at the crater's bottom, spat, and took a couple of deep breaths. He found his helmet lying beside the rotting corpse of a long-dead German, his legs, or what remained of them, half-submerged in the pool. The corpse still wore the old leather, spiked helmet from the war's opening months, and the skeletal hands emerging from its tattered and faded grey uniform still clutched a rusting rifle. A few remaining bits of flesh hung in strips from the dead man's face, and sockets long ago emptied by the carrion birds stared skyward. Daniel retched at the sight.

Somehow, the face felt familiar.

The Southern Lady

Marge Simon

With death, there should be dignity. Yet there is none here as the men in dusty blue uniforms continue to pass through our front lawns. My precious Cabbage roses are trampled, left to bleed their perfume into the soil. Half dead young men are brought to my parlor, soaking my fine couches with their Yankee blood. Old Sadie leaves her kitchen to work beside me, tending to their wounds. We must use my fine linens for bandages. They leave me no choice, though I'd certainly no plans to nurse these Union boys. Not many yesterdays ago, I fainted at the very thought of blood.

Cow and calf alike they shot for practice up in Charleston. By the time they got here, they wanted bread and butter, expected pitchers of fresh milk to wash it down. Some seem surprised to hear there's none. They'd burned our fields, there was no feed, did they think our livestock lived on love?

I dreamed I was a giant cat, sitting on a wounded soldier's chest. I watched him quietly while he slept, then I leaped on his face and clawed out his eyes. But he rose up, playing "Aura Lee" on his harmonica. One by one, his companions joined in singing, and we danced all around the room. Beyond the window it was raining blood.

The Tree of Fate and Wishes

Anthea Sharp

Emer Cuinn woke from dreams filled with blood and ashes. Her parent's voices, low and urgent, penetrated the curtained-off sleeping area of their stone cottage. Emer lay still, straining to hear over the quiet crackle of the peat fire in the main room.

"What did the council say?" Emer's mother asked.

"It's to be war." Her father sounded weary. "We march to battle in four days."

Four days? Emer sat up, her heart racing.

"Already?" Emer's mother echoed her thoughts. "But Cormac, your wound…you cannot lead the warriors out."

"A chieftain leads his men into battle." His voice was hard.

"But your second—"

"Was Sean, and his replacement is still untested. Ask me no more. I'll not shirk my duty."

Sean, thought Emer, her bright and laughing cousin Sean, his merry voice forever silenced by a blade through his chest.

Careful not to disturb her sleeping siblings, Emer rose, the flagstones cold under her bare feet. Her mother alone could not convince her father, but perhaps he would listen to their combined voices. She wrapped a woolen shawl about her shoulders and pushed open the curtain, blinking in the lantern light. Her mother looked up from the table top, caution and hope in her eyes.

"Please, father," Emer said. "Can the battle not wait?"

Although the deep slice in Cormac's thigh was healing, it had sapped him of much of his strength. On the field of war, that weakness would spell his death.

"Those troublemakers graze their cattle upon our summer fields," he said, making a fist upon the table. "Already we've waited too long. We'll drive them off, and add their herds to ours. Which will add to your dowry, lass."

She did not want a dowry bought with the clan's lives. Especially not her father's life.

"We can move our cattle..." she tried again.

"These are our lands," her father said. "Ours by right of tradition. And force, if need be."

"Go back to bed." Her mother's eyes were sad. There would be no winning the argument that night.

Or any night.

Emer withdrew to the straw-stuffed mattress, but sleep did not come. The clan would go to war in four days. The words echoed in her mind, along with a rising sense of urgency. She must *do* something. But the chieftain's daughter did not have the power to command the clan, however much she might wish it.

Wish...

The thought sparked through her, and with it came a rush of hope. She could not change the course the council had decided upon, but she could invoke the old gods. They had the power to avert the coming war.

Some distance beyond the boundaries of her clan's territory lay a sacred spring. Above the spring a hawthorn tree grew, where for generations people had come to leave their wishes, tied to the branches in the form of cloth strips and long pieces of thread. In all seasons the tree was aflutter with color and movement, the cloth braiding and unbraiding in the wind, the strands dancing in the breeze.

At the wishing tree a girl could perform small magics, beseeching the powers to grant her heart's desire, whether it be love or vengeance or greed. Or peace.

Above the hawthorn tree rose a hill crowned with a circle of standing stones. It was a place of power, and peril. The old gods slept there, and the Fair Folk were known to dance in the ring. Any mortal who offended them brought trouble down upon her head, and upon her entire clan.

One did not go lightly to the wishing tree.

But go she must, for the specter of war panted at her shoulder—a wolfhound, fierce and insatiable, sharp teeth hungry for her father's blood.

<<>>

The next day, once her chores were finished, Emer told her mother she was going to gather sweet herbs by the waterside.

"Don't stray too far," her mother said, giving her a stern look.

"I'll be careful." Emer fingered the small dagger strapped at her waist.

She collected her basket and, when her mother's back was turned, slipped an oat cake inside. One must always bring an offering to the gods when making a wish. Then she donned her blue cloak, kissed her brother and sister each upon the cheek, and set out.

At first she kept a decorous pace, but as soon as she was out of sight of the ring fort surrounding their village she gathered up her skirts and ran.

The sun shone down, the morning dew quickly drying from the grasses. The wind off the coast whipped her cloak back. She could not smell the sea—the shore and its tall gray cliffs were too far away—but she felt the weight of the ocean within the breeze.

When she tired, she slowed to catch her breath, then ran once more. She passed the stone cairn marking her clan's boundary and went more warily, though with no less haste. For a time, swallows kept her company, darting and turning above her head, but when she came closer to the spring they flew away.

The wind calmed, too, and Emer spotted the weathered circle of stones on the hill above the sacred spring. She veered so she would not come too close to that circle, adjusting her path until the gnarled branches of the hawthorn tree came between her and the hill.

The tree was in full bloom, the flowers like snow upon the green thorns. Between the drifts of white she spied the colorful tatters of strips tied to the branches. Tens and tens of wishes, left to dance in the wind and flutter beneath the stars, sending their silent prayers into the world.

At the foot of the hawthorn tree the spring lay quiet and dark. A trickle of water wove around root and stone, finally gathering itself into a small stream and meandering away around the base of the hill. The air was thick with power and possibility.

Emer stood a moment, quieting her heavy breaths. She had run far and fast to reach the tree, but it would not do to approach it panting and disheveled. The old gods deserved more than that.

"Caw!"

She started as a raven took flight from the top of the tree. Guardedly, Emer watched it sweep across the sky. One raven was a portent, but not a dire one.

Stepping carefully, she approached the tree. No more dark shapes stirred in its branches. Still, she felt invisible eyes watching her, the weight of the place folding about her. Sunlight filtered through the hawthorn branches, laying patterns of light and shadow on the grasses.

"Greetings," she said softly. "I come with a peaceful heart to ask a wish."

For this, Emer was willing, though she knew it carried a cost.

She unslung the basket from her arm and drew out the oat cake laying her offering upon a flat stone near the spring's edge.

"Please accept this small gift," she said.

Her only answer was the breeze stirring the hanging bits of cloth tied to the thorny branches. Here, beneath the tree, the sweet dusty scent of the flowers filled her nose.

Sitting, Emer worked a length of blue thread free from the hem of her cloak. She snipped it off with her small blade, then brought the thread to her lips and breathed her wish upon the strand. Once, twice, thrice she whispered the words, blowing them against the thread until it was washed in the warmth of her breath.

"Let this war be averted. Let my father grow strong and well. Let us know a time of peace, not bloodshed, between the clans."

She looked up into the tree, finding a spot to tie her wish. Bees hummed among the petals, their song sharpening as they took notice of the large, clumsy human reaching in to disturb their work.

Though she was expecting it, the first sting on her hand made her yelp. Still, she did not withdraw, but looped her string about the dark wood of a small branch.

The second sting, this time on her finger, made her breath hiss between her teeth, but she tied the first knot in the thread.

The third sting was worse than the other two combined, landing in the center of her palm. Eyes blurred with tears, Emer could barely see to wind the thread about itself. Breathing hard, she finished securing her small magic to the tree.

The moment she let go, the wind lifted the blue strand, and her heart rose at the sight, despite the pain pulsing through her hands.

Perhaps Danu would hear her wish whispering in the breeze. Perhaps the Fair Folk would carry it to the mother goddess's ears. Perhaps all was not lost.

<<>>

When Emer returned home, hands daubed with mud and a basket full of fresh herbs, her mother gave her a hard look, but said nothing. That evening Emer even had the heart to tease and sing with her siblings before the fire and went to bed with a spark of hope in her heart.

Her dreams extinguished that spark.

The sky was full of ash, and the dead lay strewn upon the trampled grass. She walked among them, afraid to gaze upon their faces, tears scorching her eyes.

"No." Emer woke with a start and clutched her blanket up to her chin.

One bit of magic was not enough. She must return to the wishing tree. Two more days, two more chances to strengthen the power of her wish before death came to eat them with its red, insatiable mouth.

I will avert this fate. She put all the force of her soul into the thought, holding it close until morning.

A new day, and warm porridge for breakfast, renewed Emer's resolve.

"Can I check the weirs for trout today?" she asked her mother.

Grainne gave her a long look, but finally nodded. "Keep out of trouble, mind."

"I'm not slipping away to meet with a boy, if that's what you fear."

"Hm." Her mother stirred the pot. "I saw the flowers Young Finn brought you last week."

Emer felt a blush warm her cheeks. "He'd given the same to Cait, the week before. I won't let the likes of Young Finn turn my head."

Though he was a handsome fellow. This last thought, however, her mother did not need to hear.

"Very well—but be home in time for supper. Especially if there's fish."

Emer kissed her mother on the cheek, then went to fetch her cloak and basket. This time, she tucked a small piece of honeycomb in alongside her oat cake.

As she had the day before, as soon as she was out of sight of the ring fort she ran. When she grew too winded, she stopped at various points to catch her breath—the hollow where bracken fern grew, the hillock overlooking a rock-strewn plain, the thicket of thorny gorse.

At last she came in sight of the hawthorn tree, the stone circle above standing sentinel. Clouds gathered overhead and the sun slipped behind them. The air suddenly carried a chill.

She paused to smooth her hair and catch her breath. Then, summoning her courage, she proceeded to the dark seep of the spring.

"I ask your indulgence again," she said to the spirits of the place, and to the old gods. "Please accept this offering."

She laid the cake upon the flat stone and put the honeycomb beside it. Her wish for peace strong within her heart, she unraveled another length of blue thread from her cloak.

“Let this war be averted,” she said. “Let my father grow strong and well. Let us know a time of peace between the clans.”

The wish welled up from her heart. She could not bear to lose her father as they had lost Sean, now buried beneath the stones. Tears escaped the corners of her eyes, and she caught them upon the thread, letting her sorrow darken the strand.

A soft breeze tickled her cheek, as if in sympathy. Perhaps the gods *were* listening.

When Emer reached up to fasten her wish upon the branch, she drew in a startled breath and froze.

There, beside her first wish, was tied a length of red thread. Fear tickled the back of her neck, and she slowly turned, peering out from the shadows beneath the tree.

Was a warrior of the enemy clan lurking nearby, ready to run her through? Or worse yet, take her hostage?

As if her fright had called it forth, a raven burst from the branches overhead, cawing sharply. Emer’s heart pounded like a drum, all her senses shouting at her to run—to abandon her wish and flee back to the safety of her own clan’s boundary.

But no. Even if she was about to be taken, she must tie her wish to the tree.

As if from nowhere, a frigid wind sprang up. The air about her turned bitter cold, and Emer’s breath plumed out in a white cloud before her face. Her fingers ached as frost swirled around them.

Moving as quickly as she could, she reached to the branch. It took several tries, her numb fingers more like twigs barely under her command than her own flesh, but at last a second blue thread hung beside the first.

The cold faded into a warm breeze and her wishes stirred, tangling and twining with the red thread: scarlet like blood, blue like the sky.

What did it mean? She shivered and backed away from the blossom-laden tree. A few petals blew down, dancing away in the wind.

And then she was away, too, running and running until she reached the cairn that marked the boundary of safety. Her hands still ached with a bone-deep cold.

It was growing twilight when she returned home, fingers chapped with cold, four fat trout from the weirs wrapped in leaves and tucked into her basket. Again, her mother gave her a hard look, but did not press.

After supper, Grainne and Cormac spoke of the coming battle, of the readiness of the clan's warriors, of the victory that must surely be theirs. The scrape of the whetstone as he sharpened his sword rasped against Emer's thoughts.

She lay awake, unwilling to fall asleep. When at last she did, ash and blood colored her dreams once more.

When she woke in the light of morning, her throat was clogged with unshed tears. Tomorrow the battle would come.

Almost, she gave up in despair. What good were her feeble wishes against the will of her father and the clan's council?

But stubbornness made her rise, and dress, and once more ask her mother if she might go out, this time to pick nettles.

"I want you close today," Grainne said. "The men are mustering, and the wind tastes of a blade's edge."

"Please." Emer's voice caught on the word. "I must go."

Three was a powerful number, everyone knew that. She must go one more time to the sacred spring, work her small magic, and tie her wish upon the tree.

"No." Her mother shook her head. "I need you to mind your siblings and keep them out from underfoot."

It was a request Emer couldn't refuse. And she would not take her brother and sister with her to the tree. Even if they could keep up, it was far too dangerous, especially with the evidence that someone else had been making their own wishes. Some enemy, wishing for her clan's downfall.

The sun crept across the sky, and Emer tended her siblings and the hearth, starting a rabbit stew and sweeping the floor. Late afternoon skimmed the sky with silver when at last her mother returned from helping provision the warriors.

"You've done well," Grainne said. "You may have your freedom until sunset—but stay close and be home by dark."

"Thank you." Emer kissed her mother upon the cheek, hoping Grainne hadn't noticed her lack of promises to obey.

She would not be able to reach the sacred spring and make the return journey before twilight lay its shadow over the land. It would be well dark by the time Emer reached home, and she surely would face her mother's wrath, but there was no help for it.

She must make her final wish.

When Grainne wasn't looking, Emer tucked an oat cake into her pouch, along with a small bottle of elderberry wine. She bid farewell to her siblings, summoned a smile for her mother, and slipped out the door.

It seemed the land fought her as she ran—her skirt tangling in the gorse, her shoes sinking into an unexpected bog, thatched clumps of grass making her stumble. At last the hill above the spring rose before her, dark against the dusk-lit sky, the stone circle crouched atop it.

Emer picked the clinging burrs from her skirt and shook it out, then approached the hawthorn tree. A bird rustled in the upper branches, causing a drift of petals, but she could not make out what it was.

Please, not a raven. A third one was proof that the Morrigan, goddess of death and destruction, would bring war to the clan on the morrow.

But war was not a certainty, not yet. Clinging to that handful of hope, Emer laid her oat cake upon the flat stone. She was not sure if she should pour out the bottle of wine as a libation, or leave all the dark liquid within the bottle.

After a moment's hesitation, she unstoppered it and poured a small measure upon the ground, then settled the bottle beside the cake.

"I bring you my small offerings," she said into the oncoming night. "Please grant my wish."

The bird rustled once more among the branches, but still did not take flight and show itself. Afraid of what she would see, she glanced up to where her first two wishes hung.

A second red thread was tied beside her wish from yesterday, and her heart clenched

She stared at the scrap of red fluttering defiantly from the thorny branch. Anger flashed hotly through her. She wanted to turn and shout into the gathering twilight, demand that whoever was there show themselves. How *dare* the enemy come here and tangle their wishes with her own?

She should abandon her foolish hope for peace, and instead use her last wish for her clan's victory in the coming battle.

Emer closed her eyes, her heart torn. The memory of her cousin Sean's death rose within her, searing and futile. It would be easy to draw on that dark, bitter well of emotion, to push it into the magic and turn her hopes from peace to war. The third wish was always the strongest.

Hadn't the interlopers stolen their lands, and even invaded the sacred space of the wishing tree? Perhaps her father was right—the only way to respond was with force. Their warriors were brave and strong. With a heartfelt plea to the Morrigan, surely her clan would prevail.

But victory came with a price. She could not wish for her father to lie upon the field, dead face staring sightless at the sky.

When she opened her eyes, she saw that the first star had appeared, a speck of light in the ash-gray sky. It was a confirmation of what was in her heart.

Despite the darkest night, there would always be stars.

Tears pricking her eyes even as the star pricked the cloak of the sky, Emer unraveled a final length of blue thread from her hem. This time, after snipping it off, she did not sheathe her small blade. Her first wish had been imbued with her breath, the second her tears. Now it was time for her blood.

Hands steady, she set the tip of the knife against her thumb and pressed until a bright drop welled. Holding her wish close to her heart, she wound the thread about her thumb and let the blood seep in.

"Let this war be averted," she said, the truth of each word ringing from the bottom of her soul. "Let my father become strong again. Let there be peace between the clans."

In the silvery twilight, she reached overhead and fastened her wish to the tree. Her thumb throbbed and the thorns on the branch scored her hands, sharp and biting, as the wishing tree took its own blood sacrifice from her. Emer bit her lip against the pain and finished tying the knot.

The breeze sprang up, pulling the thread from her fingers to dance in the wind, braiding itself with blue, red, blue, red. She withdrew her hands, the backs etched with burning scratches.

Above her, the bird took flight. For a moment all Emer could see was dark feathers, and her heart sank like a stone in deep water. A raven. A third raven. War and death would fall upon her clan on the morrow.

Then she caught a glimpse of white feathers among the black. As the bird flew away, the burbling call of a magpie reached her ears. She went to her knees in relief, the dampness soaking through her skirt, but she did not care.

She had done all she could. Now she must make her way home in the dark and face her punishment—hard words and a willow cane switching at the least. But if the gods and spirits heard her wish, it was a small price to pay.

Under the pale light of the stars and a sickle moon, she made what haste she could, but it was still two hours after sundown when she at last approached the ring fort.

"Who is it?" The guard at the gate lifted his torch, and she saw that Young Finn was on watch.

"Tis I, Emer," she said wearily. "Let me in."

"Oh, your parents are sore," he said, standing aside. "What have you been up to, out there in the dark?"

He peered into the night, as if expecting to see she'd been keeping company with someone.

"Wishing," she said.

"For victory, I hope!" His smile was white and filled with anticipation. "Tomorrow will be a glorious battle. Give me a kiss, for luck."

She brushed her lips against his cheek, but while his heart beat with red blood, hers pulsed with spring water. *Peace, peace.*

When she stepped through the door of their home, she was met with her mother's cold gaze, and her father's face set in anger.

"I know," she said, holding up her poor, abused hands. "I deserve whatever punishment you care to give me. But believe me that I have done what I had to do."

"To bed." Her father pointed to curtain wall, beyond which her brother and sister already slept. "Your punishment will come—but not this night. We must all rest and make ready for tomorrow's battle."

Emer bent her head and hurried to prepare for bed. Whatever befell her clan on the morrow, it was in fate's hands.

<<>>

Emer awoke the next morning with no memory of dreams. Predawn light sifted in through the window openings, and she felt the first stirrings of hope.

Then she turned over and saw her father strapping on his boiled leather breastplate. So. The warriors had not all woken with their desire for battle extinguished.

Surely the gods would act. Her dreams had not carried blood and ash. Did that mean the war was averted?

Quietly, she rose and dressed. She went out and helped her mother serve the men, and few fighting women, mugs of hot herbal brew. Soon after, the warriors were ready, massing at the front gate.

Emer tasted bitter hopelessness.

"I am going with the healers," she told her mother, as the noncombatants prepared to depart with the fighters. When her father fell, she would be there to tend him.

"Emer, what—"

"I am going." She grasped her mother's arms. "I must."

Grainne's dark eyes studied her. Finally, she took her daughter's face between her calloused hands.

"Be careful," was all she said, though her expression was full of love and fear and questions that Emer could not answer.

Emer shouldered a pack of supplies and set out along with the healers. In front of them, the younger warriors called cheerfully to one another, while the older men, like her father, went grimly forward. They, at least, knew that battles brought death as well as glory.

Too soon they reached the field where the chieftains had agreed to meet. The sun had risen and clawed away the mist shrouding its face. It was far too beautiful a morning for death, and Emer swallowed back the salt of her tears.

At least she would be there to bear witness as her clansmen fell. Her heart hardened against the gods as she saw the black line of opposing warriors waiting across the field. There would be no peace.

Grief aching through her body, Emer set down the pack she'd been carrying. Despite herself, her feet carried her forward until she stood at the front lines.

"Get back," Young Finn told her, with a fierce look.

Then the war pipes began to play, wailing loud as though giving voice to her anguish. Across the field, Emer glimpsed a red cloak.

"No."

She did not realize she was screaming the word as she sprinted forward. Open sky and green grass lay before her; and the faces of her enemies. Dimly, she was aware of a handful of warriors following behind her.

The opposing clan stirred, a group of them also moving onto the field.

"Come back!" her father called, but she could not.

There, as if in a mirror, a dark-haired girl in a red cloak ran across the field toward Emer, her face full of sorrow, full of hope. Behind her came her clan's warriors, until they were halted by a sharp command from their chieftain.

Closer Emer came to the stranger girl, closer, and closer still, until they met in the middle of the field.

"You," Emer gasped out. "You were wishing. Tell me—tell me, what was you wish."

"I wished for peace," the other girl said. "My name is Dierdre."

"I am Emer. And I wished the same." She could not keep a tear from slipping down her face.

"Well met, friend." Dierdre held out her hands.

They were welted with bee stings, chapped with cold, covered with scratches.

Emer stepped forward and clasped Dierdre's hands.

"Yes," was all she said.

They embraced then, and the breeze danced about them, whipping their cloaks together, red and blue.

Behind each of them, the warriors stilled and whispered. The chieftains waved their men back. Each one strode to the center of the field where their wayward daughters stood, hair tangling together, faces bright with hope.

The men halted beneath the gazes of their daughters. And their faces fell, and then rose as their eyes met. They began to speak, low and earnest. Then nodded, then a final clasping of wrists, before each turned back to their own.

There would be no war that day.

Nor was there, not for generations. Not until the last of the red thread and the blue thread frayed and faded and finally let go, whirling away from the tree into a night filled with wind, and stars, and the memory of two girls standing arm-in-arm against the tide.

A Stranger's Absolution

Al Margrave

Jimmy watched his feet as he walked along the sidewalk, hood up, hands buried in his front pockets, and shoulders hunched against the chill. The gray sky threatened rain, but he didn't care. He was on his way to see his dad, who had left four years ago.

He rounded the corner and raised his eyes to where his dad waited, past the wrought-iron fencing atop the low, white brick wall. The front gate was open and Jimmy passed through with a heavy familiarity.

He followed the main path through the headstones, hardly paying them any attention. Instead, something up ahead caught his eye—a person. The figure became clearer as Jimmy neared, an older man standing at his father's grave.

Jimmy slowed, making his steps deliberate and being careful not to drag his feet across the grass, but he wasn't quiet enough. The man turned and acknowledged him with a nod.

Jimmy glared at the man, trying to will him to leave but it didn't work.

"Hi," the man said. "You must be James."

Shocked, he answered, "Yeah. How did you know?"

"Phil used to talk about you a lot," the man said. "My name's Isaac. I served with your dad."

Jimmy studied the man. His jacket was worn, his beard thick and unkempt. The wrinkles in his tanned, weathered face suggested his edge had been dulled by the wear and tear of a life hard lived, but the gleam in his blue eyes was sharp.

Phil had returned from his third tour shortly after Jimmy turned eleven, leaving the service on a medical discharge after his Humvee was hit by a roadside bomb. Jimmy noticed right away that something about his dad wasn't quite the same. Too young to be able to put his finger on it exactly, he certainly wasn't preoccupied with figuring it out. He was just happy to have his dad home.

Over the next nine months, the changes Jimmy had only sensed at first became glaringly obvious. Phil was distant, erratic. He was quick to yell at Jimmy for small things, like leaving empty cereal bowls on the counter instead of in the sink, or having the TV turned up too loud. And he drank. A lot. Jimmy remembered backyard barbecues during the summer when his dad would have a few beers while everyone talked and laughed and ate, but he could never recall a time that he had been obviously drunk. After he came home, it was normal.

Jimmy had no idea how to adjust. He was scared of saying the wrong thing to his dad and sending him into a withdrawal or worse, a rage. His mom pulled away too. At night, he would hear his parents yelling at each other through his bedroom wall, and during the day they hardly spoke a word to each other. Dinner conversations were replaced by the sound of forks and knives on plates. Family time meant standing in a doorway watching his mom fold laundry, or sitting as still as possible on the opposite end of the couch from his dad while Phil stared blankly at the TV, only moving to lift the drink to his lips.

As if on cue, Isaac spoke again. "He was a good man. One of my best friends." He looked at Phil's headstone.

Jimmy still didn't know what to say. He was desperate to ask a thousand questions in the hope that the answers would bring him as close to his dad as this stranger was. They might even help him understand why Phil had made the decision to hang himself in the garage that day four years ago.

It was a scene he relived in dreams night after night ever since. He could see the flashing lights of the emergency vehicles in front of his house from down the block on his way home from the bus stop. His mom stood in the driveway, surrounded by paramedics and police. When she saw him, she ran to him and clutched him to her chest, her heaving sobs drowning out everything going on around them.

“He never talked about you,” Jimmy said. It was an observation more than an accusation. “He never really talked about anything after he came home.”

“I don’t blame him.” Isaac paused for a moment. “Our last deployment...”

Jimmy could tell by the sound of Isaac’s voice that the memory of something he wished he could forget was surging back to him. It was the same way Jimmy had sounded when the school counselor asked him about his dad the first time.

Isaac cleared his throat. “He talked about you all the time,” he said, the smile under his beard deepening the wrinkles at the corners of his eyes.

Jimmy shifted. He wasn’t uncomfortable talking to this man, but he was perhaps a little apprehensive about what he might learn, or what he might *not* learn. He stood there, eyes fixed on his dad’s headstone, letting his mind wander to other places as a cold breeze blew the warmth away from his face.

“What happened?” he asked. He had to take the opportunity. Anything he could learn might help.

Isaac sighed, hesitating, perhaps searching for a suitable version of the story.

“We were about halfway through our deployment,” he began, “and we got a call one night about a guy we’d been looking for, saying that he was in the area where we were patrolling. So we got our stuff together and headed to the compound where this guy was supposed to be.

“When we got there, we got lit up, guys shooting at us from everywhere. They had all kinds of stuff—machine guns, rockets, you name it. We start returning fire, and then we push up to the building and get ready to go in to clear it and look for this guy.

“So I kick the door open and your dad throws a grenade inside, and as soon as it goes off, we push in. But when we get in there, we find these bodies, a woman and these kids...” Isaac’s voice trailed off. “When we reported it, our superiors kind of brushed it off. They basically told us there was no way to know for sure if we had killed them or if they were already dead by the time we showed up, and to just keep our mouths shut and forget about it."

Jimmy's cheeks were hot now despite the cold wind, tears welling up in his eyes. He clenched his teeth, determined not to cry in front of this man, and swallowed the lump in his throat before it could rise to the top.

Isaac continued. "I remember one night a few days later, just me and your dad were in the hut, and we'd been drinking some booze we managed to score. Your dad just broke down talking about the people we found. He kept saying, 'What if it had been my wife? My kids?' I think after that he saw the shit we were doing over there a little differently. We all did."

Jimmy tried to blink the tears away but they spilled down his cheeks. He took in a shaky breath and exhaled slowly, then wiped his face. Every part of him desperately wished things had been different—that he had known what happened and could have said something to make his dad know that he loved and forgave him, or that the guy they were looking for that night had been somewhere else instead, or that his dad had never gone back for another deployment in the first place. Most of all, he wanted to scream at his dad until his throat bled and his lungs burst for leaving without giving Jimmy the chance to say goodbye.

"Probably about a month and a half later we were out on another mission, and one of our buddies—we called him Pits because he just used to sweat like crazy all the fricking time. Didn't matter what we were doing—out on a patrol or sitting around watching movies at night—this dude was constantly soaked," Isaac said, smiling a little bit as he reminisced. "He was kind of complaining because the AC was broken in the Hummer he was riding in, so Phil traded him spots. So Pits was supposed to be in the middle Hummer and your dad was supposed to be in the one in back, and they traded.

"We left the wire that day, and probably fifteen minutes into our patrol we hit an IED." He paused, his eyes fixating on a point further than either of them could see. "Pits died. He was sitting where your dad would have been. Me and him were both in the middle Hummer. It messed us up, too. He got sent home after that."

Jimmy's vision blurred as more tears flowed. He didn't care what Isaac might think of him crying anymore, or about anything else. "Why?" he asked, looking up at his dad's friend with pleading eyes. "Why didn't he ever tell us any of this? We could have helped him. We could have..." Now he was sobbing. "Maybe we could have. We could have done something. I could have told him it was okay."

Isaac stepped in and wrapped his arms around Jimmy, pulling him close in a tight hug. "I'm sure it wasn't because he didn't want to," he said. "He just didn't know how."

Jimmy got his crying under control and took a couple breaths before loosening his embrace on Isaac. Isaac let go too, and Jimmy stepped back, wiping his face with both hands.

"I was pretty tweaked from everything, too," Isaac said. "Didn't know how to talk to anyone either. Started drinking, pushing people away. Looking back at it now, I know they wanted to help, but I wouldn't let them. It cost me everything. My family, my home." He looked down at Phil's headstone, that distant stare setting in again. "Everything."

Jimmy watched as Isaac's eyes seemed to dim, and Jimmy knew that he must have struggled too. After a moment, he continued, his eyes still focused on some faraway place in his memory.

"My wife kicked me out. Said she couldn't handle it anymore. I bounced around on the streets for a couple years. Man," he said, his voice cracking slightly but just enough for Jimmy to notice, "I had no idea how hard it must have been on my son." He looked up, studying Jimmy's face and clothes, his eyes glistening. "He would have been about your age. But he couldn't—" Isaac's voice cracked again, and he broke eye contact, pausing to clear his throat—"he couldn't handle what I put him through either."

A shockwave ripped through Jimmy's chest, and suddenly he felt closer to this man than he had to anyone in his whole life. Isaac had lived through the same war that had broken his father, and he knew the tragedy of losing the person he loved the most in the world. Yet here he was, holding himself together while recounting his darkest days.

Isaac drew in a long breath. When he looked at Jimmy again, the dullness in his eyes was gone and the bright gleam had returned. “Life’s a crazy thing, man. We all have to carry our burdens. I let mine break me for a long, long time, but eventually I got to understand that it wasn’t the way I wanted to honor the people I loved.”

He reached over and squeezed Jimmy’s shoulder. The contact felt nice. Familiar. It reminded Jimmy of his dad. “But how do you stop missing them?” Jimmy asked.

Isaac’s smile tugged at the corners of his eyes. “You don’t.”

Jimmy nodded, gazing down at his dad’s headstone. *Beloved husband and father. Served his family with devotion and his country with honor. Always in our hearts.*

“You got a phone?” Isaac asked.

“Yeah.” Jimmy pulled out his cell phone and handed it to Isaac, who typed something in and handed it back.

“Here’s my number,” he said. “Call me sometime if you feel like talking.”

Isaac wished him farewell and made his way off in the opposite direction from where Jimmy had entered the cemetery. Above, the sun had finally pierced a hole in the blanket of gray clouds, casting a warm, silvery light over the rows of stones and the cool grass. Jimmy’s shoulders felt lighter as turned and began walking too. His burden would be his to carry forever, but he wouldn’t have to carry it alone anymore.

Mother of all Bombs

Lita Kurth

The Mother of All Bombs
is the mother of revenge
21,000 pounds
in mother's iron fist

The Mother of All Bombs
bestows a giant bouquet
sixteen million dollars
of smoke and steam and dust

The Mother of All Bombs
pulverizes sixty meters
of strengthened concrete walls
she flutters, floats, and falls

like ashes, the Mother of All Bombs
has a letter and a number
vaporizes bodies
crushes kidneys, livers

suffocates, the Mother of All Bombs
is the mother of all regrets
habitation turned to desert
clouds of bloody mist

The Mother of All Bombs

leaves silence in her craters
describes a two-mile circle
of no one left with hearing
no deer, no dog, no lizard.

The Mother of All Bombs
has no children, only ghosts.

Mother of All Bombs, have mercy
Mother of All Bombs, have pity
Mother of All Bombs, what you do, do quickly.

**In April, 2017, the U.S. dropped "the Mother of All Bombs" on a site in Afghanistan.*

Remembrance Day

Liam Hogan

The comm icon flashes and my finger hovers over it for a long moment before I tap. It's Doctor Reynolds and I feel the edge fade from the tension that's been building all morning.

He nods, the computer generated pixels blurring as he does. "Samuel, it's time," he says in his soothing voice.

My trembling fingers fumble with the pill box and it seems to take an eternity before I manage to free the little yellow pill. I swallow it down with a gulp of cold coffee and open my mouth wide to show that it is gone.

The simulation nods again. "Thank you, Samuel. Have you decided where you will attend?"

I shrug. "St Margaret's, I think. It's closest."

"Good, good." There's a gentle smile on the Doctor's face as he reaches out a CGI hand towards an imagined keyboard and with a: "Keep well, Samuel", he signs off.

I close down my work session. There's no point in doing any more today, though I still have the best part of half an hour to kill. As I change my shirt and tie, I catch a glimpse of my uniform at the back of the wardrobe, hidden and protected by its plastic sheath. Should I be wearing it? Somehow it doesn't feel right, so I leave it hanging there. But I do dig out my medal box and it surprises me once again to see how many there are. What, I wonder, are they all for?

Because, of course, I don't remember the War.

There's one medal I do recognise though; the one my father had, the Purple Heart. I wonder where I was wounded. There are no obvious signs, except for a livid patch of scarred tissue on the palm of each hand. My father lost a leg in the Middle East. What did I lose?

I'm beginning to feel the nerves return and I take an eternity in the bathroom, neatening my hair, fussing over my tie. It's too warm and I can already feel sweat trickling down my arm. I splash cold water onto my face, think about changing the shirt, but a glance at my watch warns me I'm cutting it fine, so I grab my keys and begin the brisk walk to the church.

The sidewalks are thick with people, all in their mid-thirties to early forties—my age—and all heading the same way. A few of them are wearing uniforms: khaki, or navy blue. A few I recognise. I wonder if I served with any of them.

We file into the church, which today, at least, is full. I didn't realise there were this many Veterans in town. I find a space towards the back. The man who moves up to make room for me grins nervously and proffers his hand. "Richard O'Connor," he says. The hand is slick with sweat.

"Samuel Adams," I reply.

He pauses before letting go. "What, like the beer?"

No, like the man, do you really think my father would name me after a beer? But I don't say that. I simply nod.

He nods back. "A pleasure to know you, Sam. Any idea where you served?"

"No. You?" I ask.

He shakes his head. "I thought of looking it up, but..."

But of course he didn't. Like everyone else, his memory stops at the start of basic training and continues the day he returned home. We're warned that any memories we do accidentally awaken might be painful, or even dangerous, so we don't go looking. Trained as we are not to dig too deep, some people say Vets lack drive and ambition. That we're not "All we can be."

I don't know about that.

My ex-wife Cathy couldn't understand why I went through with the treatment. "Those who forget are doomed to repeat," she quoted, "and the War isn't just about the soldiers. It was harsh on us as well, but if it is to mean anything at all, we have to live with the decisions that were made and learn from them."

I told her she was wrong. That it didn't have to mean anything, that she didn't have to live with it and she didn't need to go on her little marches, her pointless peace rallies. The treatment was available to Service wives and husbands. To anyone who felt they had been a victim of the War. Look what it has done for me, I said.

She hadn't liked that. It got ugly and she left, claiming I wasn't the man she once knew.

The screen at the end of the church is showing a field of poppies, swaying in the wind. It looks fuzzy, low quality, and I wonder when and where it was filmed. There's a bang behind me and I feel my heart pound in my chest, but it's merely the big wooden doors being closed. Facing forward again, I see the poppies have been replaced by the craggy, worn features of Bob Tyler, the Vice-President.

"Today, we honor our soldiers," he solemnly intones. "All of those who served; the living and the dead. We come together to recognise the sacrifices you have made and to apologise." He leans forward over his clasped hands and lowers his head.

"We apologise for demanding the impossible of you. We apologise for not knowing how to cope, when the War was over and you returned, damaged, needing our support, our patience, and our compassion. The actions we took to end the War—actions that we asked you to follow through—were horribly divisive. We were shocked, when we realised that even in victory, our great nation might tear itself apart, and the returning Veterans, who should have been treated as heroes, became instead an intolerable reminder of those difficult decisions."

Tyler looks up again, his eyes reddened. "And so we asked you to make one more sacrifice. We asked that you forget."

"We were desperate, so we told you that we could make your pain and suffering go away. The vast majority of you accepted us at our word and took Doctor Reynold's procedure: a combination of hypnosis and psychotropic drugs that allowed you to lock away all memory of the War." He pauses. "But that vault is only as strong as you make it and it must be renewed. That is why, each Remembrance

Day these past fifteen years, we have asked you to step forward once again.

"On the eleventh chime of the eleventh hour, you will remember. A short while later, another bell will sound, the signal for your hypnotic suggestions to kick back in and, aided by the drug you took this morning, you will once again forget. By tomorrow, you will even forget the remembering."

Tyler looks at the clock behind him. "Once more then, I salute you, you and your continued service. On behalf of the President, the Chiefs of Staff, and the whole country, I sincerely apologise for what you are about to re-experience."

The Vee-Pee bows his head as the first of the chimes echoes out through the speakers. I sit, gripping the edge of my seat, trying to understand what he's just said. Had the country really been on the brink of civil war? How could I not have been aware of that?

Cathy though... I remember her coming home from a march, dirty, frightened, asking to be held. Long hours we lay, her face turned away, her body shivering. When I awoke sometime around dawn, still wearing yesterday's clothes, her place in the bed was empty, the sheets ruffled and damp, and from the bathroom I heard the shower on full blast. She never talked about it and I never asked. I fumble with the box in my pocket as the chimes continue to ring out.

And then—

When I come to it is to the echo of a bell ringing faintly in my ears, my body wrecked with tension, tears drying on my cheeks. I unfurl my fists and look dully at the blood oozing from the crescents my nails have cut deep into the already scarred palms.

By my feet, Richard O'Connor lies half in the pew, half in the aisle, cradling his arm and whimpering. Nearby there's a guy who works at the hardware store staring stupidly at his tattered uniform, his face and hands heavily scratched. As I watch, his legs crumple and he falls in slow motion. The church doors have been opened again and a nurse rushes to his side.

I can feel my memories of the War fading, already some I recall only as in a newscast, as if I hadn't actually been there. But I remember the first atrocity: the burning, suffocating gas. Six months I spent in hospital as they re-grew the lining of my lungs.

I remember returning to the front line and how desperate things had become by then, the terrible loses we had incurred. The prayers that if we just held on a little longer, the tide might turn.

And I remember the yellow and black labels on the syringes we were ordered to inject, on the last day of the War, a day when not a shot was fired.

The morning after we were briefed; we had a humanitarian task to perform. It was difficult to comprehend. We'd been fighting for our lives, our very survival, and now we were supposed to go into the enemy's trenches and offer medical assistance to the injured? We were warned that in some cases, our humanitarian aid might involve the use of our handguns. There were murmurs of approval.

But there were no survivors, not that day. The dead... it's fading fast, but I do remember the smell. I feel nauseous and I clutch the side of the pew to stop myself from falling. An arm gently pushes me back onto the hard seat, fleeting fingers on my wrist feeling the pulse before moving on.

I remember the radios hissing static, the blackened tins atop primus stoves long burnt out. We pressed on. Beyond the command bunkers, we entered the first of the villages, where the odd shaped piles didn't wear uniforms, and some—many—were hardly bigger than my kit bag.

We camped in an open field that night, trying to escape the stench that had intensified throughout the day. I don't remember what we did, what we said. I remember Wilkins swearing at a pair of cows: how dare they be alive, he ranted, he'd soon fix that—bang, bang... bang.

The third shot was for himself.

I think I remember our first survivor, two days and thirty miles beyond the front, begging me to use my pistol. After that, the twisted, inhuman faces merge into one nightmare vision of pain and suffering. I remember running out of ammo and unbuckling my knife, the knife my father gave me, the knife I left behind.

I never did get to use the medical kit. By the time we got to people who could be saved, helicopters were already there, ferrying them out. There was no room for us and our grumbles earned us black looks from the medics. We went back the way we came, avoiding the silent villages.

I realise I've left the church, though I can't recall having done so. There are bloodstained strips of gauze wrapped around my hands and I'm standing on a bridge, holding my medal box by the corner as if it were poisonous. Perhaps it is. If I dropped it into the grey waters below, I think I know what would happen. In a week or so I'd get a note from the local jewellers thanking me for my custom and the medals would be returned, polished and pristine, this moment, like the whole goddamn war, wiped clean. I slip them back into my pocket and begin the weary walk home.

I'm done remembering, and I can't wait for this day to be forgotten.

Valor

Gwyndyn T. Alexander

The warriors feast
before the shattered walls
of the devastated city.

They drink their stolen wine,
wallow in the looted riches,

and celebrate their victory
with the rape of the city's women.

The buildings still burn fitfully.
The ruins smolder.
The shopkeepers' bodies rot
quietly in the sun.

The victors stroll through the broken streets,
kicking the corpses of children
out of their path.

Chained together,
the women sit bleeding,
torn and violated,
too stunned to grieve.

After the debauch of celebration,
the soldiers bicker over the wedding rings,
heart's lockets, and heirlooms

they have stripped from the dead.

A woman sits silent,
tears falling unnoticed, even by her,
as her husband's body is searched for hidden jewels,
then tossed onto the pyre.

She is chattel, now.
She is flesh to be used and discarded,
in the ashes of her home,
among the bodies of her dead.

There are no wails, no screams, no words.

The women are mute in their agony,
lost in their grief.

Among the men, there is much laughter,
and singing, and quarrels over loot.

When they are done with their rapine,
they will move on to the next town,
to do it all again.

They will slaughter the women
before they go,
or sell them to be used.

The women watch,
voiceless, nameless,
their blood quietly seeping into the ground
they had nurtured, and tilled,
the seeds now scattered, the crops trampled
and fouled and defiled.

It is the season for men to go to war.
It is always that season.

The women sit, and count their dead,
and cradle the limp, silent children who will,
at least, cry no more.

The victorious hero is feted, cheered,
carried on the shoulders of his warriors.

His name will live forever.

Tamerlane, Sherman, MacArthur. Alexander.

We know them.
We build them shrines.
We tell their stories.
We wave their flags.

The women, the children,
they fade into the blood soaked soil,
forgotten, unknown, unmourned.

They are the spoils, awarded to the victor,
then casually discarded.

The men keep the trinkets, and throw away
what has no worth, no value.

The women.
The children.
The lifetimes of memories.
The history.

The only stories that matter
are those of the conquering heroes.

Women are prizes.
Women are targets.
Women are disposable.

But we women know.
We know the stories of the lost.
We know our place.

There are no victories for us.
There are no monuments, no songs,
no parades.

We are the acceptable losses.
We are the casualties,
with the emphasis on 'casual'.

We know the truth of war.
We know the truth of glorious battle.
We know the truth
of heroes.

Welcome to HomeDrone

Shawn Kobb

Dear Valued Customer,

Welcome to HomeDrone(™)!

We appreciate you joining us in this exciting new adventure. No longer will you be forced to wait days for your valuable purchases. Thanks to HomeDrone's(™) extensive network of corporate partnerships, intelligent warehousing, and high-speed AI-enhanced drones, the future is here...today!

Within milliseconds of your confirmed purchase, our workers (both organic and robotic) get to work on your order. We identify the closest distribution center and within 90 seconds, your purchase is packaged, loaded, and departs our warehouse on one of our patented rapid delivery HomeDrones(™).

Once you have experienced the joy and convenience of near instantaneous home delivery you'll wonder how you ever lived before.

HomeDrone
The future is now! (™)

Dear Valued Customer,

We are extremely sorry to hear about your ongoing problem with package theft. As you may have heard, HomeDrone(™) is experiencing challenges with new entrants into the drone home delivery sector. Unfortunately, not every company adheres to the strict customer-centric code of ethics that is at the heart of HomeDrone(™). We are confident the courts will rule in our favor in the near future, and theft from rival drones will cease.

In the meantime, we are pleased to announce a new program designed to ensure the safety of your deliveries. Our new DecoyDrones(™) will operate seamlessly alongside our HomeDrones(™) to deliver your valuable household goods quickly, securely, and reliably.

Thanks to our advanced Predictive Proprietary Logistics Management System, the DecoyDrones(™) will prevent future theft to the greatest extent possible.

You have been automatically enrolled in the DecoyDrone(™) program at no additional cost.

We appreciate your patience during this time. As with any new and innovative technology, certain roadbumps are to be expected. Together, we shall overcome these temporary challenges.

HomeDrone
The future is now! (™)

Dear Favored Customer,

Although we share in your disappointment of our judicial system's failure to put an end to the blatant theft of our technology, and more importantly, the disruption of our uniquely reliable delivery to you, our valued customer, HomeDrone(™) continues to work every day to adapt to a rapidly changing situation.

The DecoyDrone(™) program has been an unquestionable success. HomeDrone(™) deliveries completed in tandem with DecoyDrones(™) have resulted in a decrease of 73 percent in package theft.

Unfortunately, due to inferior technology utilized by our competitors, our DecoyDrones(™) appear to be triggering a counter deployment of "raider" drones. This escalation has resulted in the "insane maelstrom of drones" you have reported above your residence.

We appreciate your patience as we navigate the challenges of this new age. We will continue to fight this battle both in the courts as well as through the development of exciting new technologies. Please stay tuned for exciting news on this front very soon!

In the meantime, we are pleased to provide you a $50 credit toward future HomeDrone(™) delivered products as well as a $25 gift card which you can share with a friend.

Thank you for your continuing support and patronage.

HomeDrone
The future is now!(™)

Dear Premium Patron,

Exciting news! HomeDrone(™) is pleased to announce the newest in autonomous vehicle delivery technology: DefenderDrone(™)!

Tired of your valuable household supplies being pilfered by rival drones?

Concerned your hard-earned dollars are at risk due to the reckless actions and immoral decisions of faceless figures hiding behind their big fancy desks in Who Knows Where? Russia? China? Australia??

Disgusted that the legal system of your nation has failed you in your God-given right to expedient home delivery?

DefenderDrone(™) promises to restore order and decency to the world of convenient home delivery. Showcasing the most advanced technology from the HomeDrone(™) design lab, the DefenderDrone(™) is sheathed in titanium plating for durability, nitrox-boosted propulsion for agility, and small caliber hollow-tipped ammunition for superior anti-drone stopping power that poses minimal risk to ground-based organic life.

It's a win-win-win!

Because of your long-standing loyalty to HomeDrone(™), you have automatically been enrolled in the DefenderDrone(™) program. Your DefenderDrone(™) will self-deliver within 48 hours. No action is needed on your part. The DefenderDrone(™) is pre-programmed and will take all appropriate and necessary action.

HomeDrone
The future is now!(™)

Dear HomeDrone Patriot,

During these difficult times in drone-based home delivery, it is important to remember one thing: We're All in This Together(™).

They thought they could steal from our HomeDrones(™).

They thought they could outsmart the superior protection provided by DecoyDrone(™).

Now they think they can out-gun the DefenderDrone(™)?

Have no doubt. We stand arm in arm with you, our valued customer. Together we say, "Not on our watch! Not today, not ever!" Your right to timely and secure home delivery WILL NOT be infringed upon.

It's clear the courts do not value the importance of convenient home delivery. Are they in the pocket of inferior home-delivery drone rivals? It's impossible to say. We leave that up to our customers to decide. As you said in your recent correspondence, "This is insanity!" We couldn't agree more.

Let us be clear: we've heard your concerns about the rapid, reliable delivery of your orders.

As impressive as the offensive might of our DefenderDrones(™) may be, it is clear they can't do it alone. Because of this undeniable fact, we have exciting news.

Due to your prolonged and unflinching loyalty, we have automatically enrolled you in our new ThunderDrone Autonomous Home Defense Matrix(™). That's right! At no additional cost, we're deploying our new state of the art delivery defense system to your location.

No action is required on your part. The system is self-erecting, self-loading, and fully guided with the most advanced threat-targeting technology on the market today.

It's just our little way of saying thank you.

We have also noted your request to suspend pet supplies. Please accept our thoughts and prayers in this time of loss. The advanced organic detection system in the Thunderdrone module will preclude any future events.

HomeDrone
The future is now!(TM)

Patriot 7G42,

The tide is turning.

The courts would not listen? They lie in ruins, the blood of millions on their hands.

The enemy infringes upon our territory? We shatter their feeble attempts through the might of our advanced technology, superior intelligence, and loyal customer base.

We at HomeDrone(™) value your unwavering support and thank you for trusting us with your home delivery needs.

Your stockpiles will automatically be replenished every four to six hours per your terms of service. During replenishment, it is highly recommended that all organics remain inside designated HomeDrone Shelter Space(™). Failure to do so could disrupt necessary functions of your HomeDrone Neuro-Kinetic Mech Sentinel(™) and may result in unintended death and/or dismemberment.

As always, thank you for your loyalty in this struggle for superior convenience in home delivery.

HomeDrone
The past, the present, and the future! For eternity!(™)

The Changeling

Tom Howard

The dry wind danced around them as the old man and his granddaughter walked down the lane. Overhead, three pale moons hung in the orange sky.

"Grandpa," she said after a long pause, "I love you."

The old man smiled. The seven-year-old had a habit of filling empty spaces in conversation with whatever popped into her head. He didn't mind. He enjoyed spending time with her and walking across the family land on a sunny afternoon.

He squeezed her hand carefully. Soon she'd be too grown up for butterfly kisses and long walks across the field with her grandfather. "Flower Girl, I love you to Triton and back."

Philomena giggled.

They paused to watch the cattle grazing. When he'd first arrived on the Perditius colony, he'd never imagined his family would someday raise Earth cattle on it. After backbreaking toil and an unexpected war with the neighbors, they had survived to enjoy the fruits of their labors.

"Ten times to Triton." She released his hand, pointed to the moon under discussion, and spun around him on her tiptoes.

"Ten times!" her grandfather exclaimed. "Are you learning multiplication in school already?"

"I'm not a baby, Grandpa." Her large amber eyes grew wide, as though with indignation, but her expression quickly shrouded with a new thought, and she frowned.

"Did something happen at school this week?" he asked.

She nodded. "I hurt Jimmy." She showed the old man her hand, exposing her small black claws. "We were playing tag, and I reached for him and... He had to see the school nurse."

Grandpa leaned on his cane. His leg, injured in the war, hadn't been the same even after the army docs repaired it. "Did you hurt him on purpose?"

"No, Grandpa!"

He smiled. "It's all right then. That's why we call them accidents. I'm sure he'll be fine. I did something similar to a boy playing water polo on Earth. I sliced his back so bad he had to leave the pool."

"Pool?" She stared at him. "You mean dipping your body in water?" She shuddered, and the old man refrained from stroking her head. With her crest coming in, he might hurt his own hand and make her feel worse.

"Your grandmother used to say I could open tin cans with these." He held his tiny pink fingernails out for her to see.

She looked thoughtful. "Grandpa..."

Here it comes.

"Why don't I look like you and Mama and Daddy?"

He smiled.

"Don't some of the other children in your class look different from their mothers and fathers?"

"Yes, some of them look like me," Flower Girl told him. "But why?"

"It's a long story," he said. "Let's find a cool spot, and I'll explain."

She looked down the road. "Who's that?"

He shaded his eyes. "I don't see anyone." His old eyes were no match for her youthful reptilian ones. "Could it have been a colinx? Your Uncle Bradley said he's cleaned them out of the valley."

"They scare me. Cousin Jeri says they gobble up a calf in one gulp. And they love little girls."

Grandpa laughed. "You shouldn't listen to Jeri's stories." He squinted down the road. "Maybe you saw a colinx."

"No," she said. "It was someone walking."

"Maybe a traveler passing through. They'll be coming up the road soon. In the meantime, let's sit here. I could use a rest." He pulled a canteen out of his pocket and opened it before offering it to Philomena. "Water?"

"No. Thank you, Grandpa." Her small body required much less moisture than his, but his thirst gave him an excuse to search for the right words for *The Talk*. That was a job for her parents, but he couldn't lie to her.

He looked over the grasslands as he drank, impressed with the tough plants able to survive without rain. All the moisture the plants required came each night on low-lying fog banks. The early colonists had built wind traps to gather the dew for themselves and their livestock, traps still used today.

He settled himself on a rock wall, and she climbed up beside him.

"Tell me why, Grandpa."

He picked up two round stones. "On the other side of our sun, there's a planet much like Perditius. It's a little hotter and a little drier, but people live there."

"Agera," she said. "Teacher told us."

"Did he tell you we came here to Perditius from far, far away?"

"Yes. From Ter-Ra, but you call it Earth."

"Terra, that's right. We came on a sleeper ship, thousands of us. We thought we'd found the perfect world." He spread his arms wide to indicate Perditius.

"I like it," Philomena said.

"Me, too." He set a rock down and put his arm around her shoulders. He looked at the other rock. "The Agerians claimed Perditius for themselves even though they lived on the other side of the sun and ignored it. We fought a terrible war to convince them we belonged here."

"Is that when Grandma died?" she asked.

"Yes, and many others."

"What does this story have to do with why I don't look like you?"

"Ah," he said. "You're too smart for your own good. You get that from me. Along with your stubbornness, according to your mother."

Stones rattling behind them distracted him, and he stood, grabbing his cane. The pasture and the road were empty. Whoever Philomena had seen must have cut across the fields. He smiled at his nervousness and sat down, one stone still in his hand.

She waited for him to continue.

"Since you've already heard the story of how we got here," he said, "I'm going to tell you a different story. A Terran one."

She nodded.

"Once upon a time, there lived a powerful king who, whenever he conquered neighboring kingdoms, killed the old kings and adopted their sons to raise them as his own."

"And daughters?" she asked.

"I'm sure he adopted the daughters, too. Do you know why he raised them as his own?"

She shook her head.

"So that when they grew up, they'd love him and not blame him for their parents' deaths. If he'd killed the children, the people would've risen up against him. This way, he had princes loyal to him."

Philomena frowned. "I don't understand. Why don't I look like you?"

"Well," Grandpa said, "think of yourself as a little princess, growing up in a new family."

Her eyes grew wide. "You killed my father?"

Grandpa chuckled. "No. When the war with Agera became too destructive and it looked as if neither side would survive, we made a peace agreement. To ensure we kept it, we agreed to exchange some of our children. We were lucky enough to get you."

"Mama isn't my mama?" She looked hurt.

"Of course, she is. Just like your dad is your dad, and your grandpa is the best grandpa in the whole wide world. It's not who gives birth to you that make them your parents. It's who kisses you and tickles you and makes you study and do your chores. It's the people who love you."

She considered it. "So, my mama is my new mama?"

"Yes, and she loves you almost as much as I do."

"What happened to her real baby?" she asked.

"That boy went to Agera to be with his new family, not the same one you came from. He's being raised and loved there as you are raised and loved here."

"Will I have to go back?"

He shook his head. "Nope. You're here forever and ever. I expect to walk your grandchildren down this road someday."

He could see her thinking it over, but a sound behind him made him sit up straighter. Something cold and hard pressed against his throat.

"Don't move, or you'll be dead before you hit the ground." The accent was Agerian.

Philomena screamed and slid off the wall. She didn't run but stood with her hands over her mouth.

"Come to me, child," the voice ordered.

She didn't move. "You let my grandpa go!"

The blade eased away slowly, and Philomen rushed into his arms. Shielding her with his body, Grandpa turned to see an Agerian. The alien, his crest extended and a bright crimson, was too young to have fought in the colonial wars. His rusty and dented armor had to be a souvenir from his father or grandfather, and his blade appeared thin and ornamental.

"What do you want?" Grandpa asked.

"I've come for my child."

"Are you mad? We swore to uphold the Covenant."

The Agerian growled. "My Covenant is broken. My wife is dead. The changeling boy we had, too. Since I no longer have a child, I've come to take mine back."

Grandpa looked the alien in the face. "What happened to them?"

"A vehicle accident."

Grandpa felt the alien's pain. "I'm sorry, but you cannot take my granddaughter."

The alien bared his fangs and reached for Philomena.

"No!" she screamed and struck him. Her claws sliced down the back of his hand, and he drew back in surprise.

Grandpa shoved the blade away with his cane and swung the rock he still held at the Agerian's head. His cane, made of titanium alloy, blocked the blade, and the rock connected with the attacker's right temple. Grandpa pushed off the wall and pulled Philomena behind him.

The Agerian wiped orange blood from the side of his head. "Look at her, old man. She's not soft like you. She needs to be with her own people."

Philomena clutched Grandpa and peeked around his overalls.

"Is this how you treat family?" Grandpa asked. "You're scaring her. I lost my wife in the war. But stealing Philomena won't bring anyone back. She is *my* granddaughter."

"I am Gratok, her father!" the alien shouted.

"Your government hasn't broken the Covenant. You have. Taking her from me won't be easy. I survived the battle at TweeSoon. Flower Girl, run for home."

Philomena ran up the road but stopped and turned to watch as Gratok approached her grandfather.

Gratok grasped a round sphere from his belt, a rusted percussion grenade, and tossed it at the old man.

"Grandpa!" Philomena shouted and ran back to him.

"No!" Grandpa shouted, with no time to grab her up and carry her to safety, ignored the pain in his bad leg and ran to put himself between the grenade and his granddaughter and fell on the grenade before it stopped rolling.

When Philomena reached him, he still lay huddled atop the grenade. It hadn't gone off.

The alien rose from his cover behind the wall. Clearly baffled, he stared at Grandpa. "You threw yourself on the bomb when you saw her returning. It would have killed you."

"What else could I do?" Grandpa sat up, wary of the unexploded ordnance, but unable to rise quickly without assistance. "She's my granddaughter."

The Agerian shook his head. "I didn't move to save her. I worried more for my own safety than hers."

"Putting someone else's well-being ahead of your own is the definition of family," Grandpa said.

Gratok stepped forward.

Philomena leaped in front of her grandfather with a stone in her hand. "Stay away from my grandpa!"

"Be still, little one. I will not harm him." Gratok helped the old man to his feet and away from the grenade. "The Covenant will not be broken. Tell the authorities what you will, old man." His crest flattened against his skull, a sign of defeat and submission.

"This?" Grandpa glanced at the dud grenade. "This never happened."

The Agerian nodded and turned away.

"Wait, Gratok," Grandpa said. "Can you find your way back to this spot on Philomena's birthday?"

The Agerian's crest raised. "Yes."

Grandpa hugged his granddaughter to him. "We will set a place for you at the table."

"What about the Covenant?" Gratok asked.

"The Covenant says nothing about who I invite to my granddaughter's birthday party."

Gratok picked up his blade and gave Philomena one last look. "Thank you."

Grandpa watched him walk down the road before leaning on his granddaughter and limping toward the ranch. He'd send someone to destroy the grenade.

Looking down at Philomena, he said, "A hundred times."

"Grandpa! That's not fair. I wasn't ready."

After a few minutes, she said, "What comes after a hundred?"

Rags of Peace

Vlora Konushevci

The spring of '99 forgot to blossom,
I vaguely remember others or the light
but there was darkness, rain, desolation
and auto bombs
exploding in Tophane at night,
Rakovica's basement at the end of an alley,
my mother's eyes, those bogey slaves and
tanks across the street.

I smuggled some rags of peace in a backpack
from the memories I carefully gathered
as shells in a shore, to remind me
of myself, as war they said, makes you forget
who you are.
In the shirt I was wearing my mother sewed up
two small pads where she hid the phone
numbers of freedom, to find each other as
war, they said, loses your trace.

My backpack, the queen of peace, crowned
with smiles in the photo album,
crushed, dragged and squeezed in the train wagons
to Bllace, pretty as a wild flower full of life,
embedded as a winter behind me, defied the
suffocation
in the wagons as a battle shield,
as Rakovica's shelter, as the blazing sun

on the bleak face of
the border.

As the lute opens to sing to the brave
so did my queen cheerfully open,
peace arrived while we waited at the border camps
as I unpacked the rags for those
whose rags were lost,
and shared them
just as a mother shares her bread
with her youngsters.

*Tophane—A neighborhood at the center of the old part of Prishtina capital of Kosovo.
*Rakovica—A family name, the family which sheltered over 100 residents in their basement.
*Bllace—the border area with Macedonia where refugee camps were built for Kosovars expelled from their homes.

War Zone

David Gerrold

President Bourget was having tuna salad for lunch when the Chief of Staff strode in, followed by two Secret Service men. He looked grim.

"We have a situation," he said.

"Crap," she said, her fork poised in mid-air. She took the bite anyway, wiped her mouth, then pushed herself away from the table. "Let's go." She reached for her cane.

She followed them to the elevator that would take them down to the Situation Room. "Get State," she said. "And the Joint Chiefs, and where's Zimmer?"

"She's on her way. And Intelligence too."

Two guards stood by the door to the Situation Room. They saluted as the President approached. She nodded to them. "Thank you." It wasn't standard protocol, but President Robbie Bourget never ignored anyone. She acknowledged everyone she encountered. The political cartoonists had her shaking hands with dogs, cats, and even the Thanksgiving turkey.

The door whooshed open, revealing the serious-looking men and women in the room. She went directly to the head of the table. "This better be good," she said, carefully taking her seat. "I was having a very nice tuna salad." She handed her cane to an aide. "All right." She looked up at the main display that dominated the far end of the room. The screen showed a regional map, spotted with military and naval resources. She said, "The Mideast, right? What now?"

Admiral Joel Landon, gray-haired and stocky—he moved with an air of methodical competence—gestured to an assistant, who tapped a control. The display now showed a man in a black ski-mask, angrily shouting into the camera. “He’s saying ‘Death to America,’” the Admiral began.

“I don’t need a translator. I recognize that phrase.” She looked around the table and added, “the word is death, but the cultural context is different. It’s just his way of saying ‘Fuck America.’ Ignore it. It’s just noise. Red meat for the home audience. Okay, now that I’ve said that, who are they and what do they want?”

Before anyone could answer, the screen flashed to show an image of destruction—orange flames rose high against the darkness of night, illuminating a cloud of thick black smoke and silhouetting an unidentifiable city. Admiral Landon had a headphone held to his right ear. He wasn’t the only one listening to the distant voices. Others around the darkened room also had headsets and earpieces. The Admiral said, “Okay, it’s confirmed. They hit our embassy in Baghdad.”

“Who’s the guy in the ski-mask?”

Paul Simpson, The Acting Director of National Intelligence stepped forward and said, “We’re working on voice identification now. He claims to be a member of Altahrir AljadidIt means ‘New Liberation.’ It’s a splinter faction of a splinter faction. They’ve been on our radar for a year or two, but we haven’t considered them a serious threat—”

“Until now. You’d better take a long hard look at what you missed and why.” The President took a deep breath. She nodded toward Admiral Landon. “Do we have a casualty report yet?”

Admiral Landon answered, “Too soon, Ma’am. I’ll have—wait a minute.” He bent his head as he listened to something on his headset. “The top two floors are gone. Ground floor is ... not good. We don’t know if the basement levels survived. It looks like a missile, not a car bomb.”

“Where’d they get the missile? Find out. How many people would have been onsite?”

“Let me address that,” Simpson said, referring to the tablet he held. “If they had hit us during the day, the casualties would have been our day staff and local civilians applying for travel visas. But we also have diplomatic services and part of our intelligence operation situated in the building as well. But it's past eight, so most of the day staff would have gone home. I have to say, Madam President, the timing is unusual. Terrorists usually want a high death count."

"Go on," she said.

"It's too early to be certain, we're still gathering intel, but it looks like they wanted to minimize casualties while crippling our local operations. That's not terrorism. Not as we know it. This is something else—"

"It's war," said the Secretary of Defense, striding into the room. All eyes turned to him. Even the President. She turned in her chair to look.

Secretary of Defense Stephen Garinger was a tall imposing man with an unruly mane of silver hair. "It's asymmetrical war," he said, taking his seat at the table. "Good morning, Madam President. I was briefed on the way over. Here's the thing. The embassy is considered American soil. So we have to consider this attack as serious as 9/11."

President Bourget said, "I'm not going to consider anything until I have all the information—"

Admiral Landon straightened. He looked grim. "Ma'am? We have a casualty estimate. There was a reception scheduled, there were nighttime meetings as well. There were negotiations in progress. The building was near fully staffed. The death toll could be as high as 300. There would have been top level government officials and leaders of the business communities as well. Our ambassador—"

"Shit," said the President. And after that, a long string of words in Spanish, several in German, and she finally concluded with a simple declaration in French. *"Merde."* She buried her face in her hands for a moment. Seated around the table and lined up against the walls, the occupants of the room waited silently for her to recover her composure.

Finally, she looked up. "Talk to me. What else do we know?"

Acting-Director Simpson spoke up. He'd been listening to his own headset. "It wasn't The New Liberation that hit the embassy. That's a false flag." He waved at the screen. "Whoever that is—" He pointed to the screen where the figure in the ski-mask, was a frozen image, "—he's just a distraction, a small-time player, pretending he's a boss. Here's what we think. The missile was likely a Zhukin-III. The Iranians bought six of them from Russia. They shipped them roundabout through half a dozen ports and ships, passing them through several sets of hands and multiple manifests—they even shipped a few decoys, here and there. They did everything they could to muddy the chain of ownership, but six Zhukins ended up in a warehouse just outside of the Iranian port of Chabahar. We had it under surveillance, both on the ground and high-altitude reconnaissance. Two of the missiles shipped out two weeks ago, but there was a major sandstorm and we lost track of them. We spotted some suspicious activity in the Gulf, but confidence was low. Even with the best of our technology, there are still limits. This missile was most likely launched from a disguised fishing boat. We're checking that now."

The President shook her head in annoyance. "All that expensive technology, and a sandstorm...? All right, at least we know what we're dealing with. And maybe who." She looked to Admiral Landon. "How good is your surveillance? Can you find that boat? Can you identify it with confidence? And can you sink it?"

"Yes, Madam President. There isn't a seagull that farts in the Gulf that we don't know about it. And we have drones in the air 24/7. We can find that boat—and we can put it on the ocean floor."

"Thank you. If I ever need to know about seagull farts, I'll call you."

Admiral Landon nodded. "Yes, Ma'am." He beckoned one of his aides and began quietly issuing instructions.

"All right." President Bourget looked around the table, making eye contact with each of the directors, the military heads, and the cabinet members present. "So, is this a consensus—that the real author of the attack on our embassy is Iran?"

Silence.

"Does anyone want to suggest any other bad actors?"

More silence.

Finally, Garinger, the Secretary of Defense, interrupted. "Madam President, we need to respond."

President Bourget leaned back in her chair, waiting. "Sinking a fishing boat isn't enough?"

"No," said Secretary Garinger. "We need something much more definitive."

"What are you suggesting?"

"We have a number of scenarios for just such a situation. The most practical is a naval blockade."

"I'm not in favor of putting any of our big expensive aircraft carriers in range of their planes or missiles. Especially not their missiles."

"We don't have to. We have two carriers within striking range. We can take out their radar first, then their airfields. Then as many of their military bases as necessary."

"How many do you think are necessary?"

"All of them," said the Secretary of Defense.

"Let's table that thought," said the President. She leaned forward again. "I'm not going to ad-lib us into a war." She looked around. "Where's the Secretary of State?"

An aide replied. "Still enroute, Ma'am."

"I need her here. I want her input."

"Yes'm."

The President turned to the Director of National Intelligence. "You have that look on your face. Tell me what you're thinking."

"Thank you, Ma'am. I'm thinking about context. If the missile came from Russia, then what was their intention in selling it to Iran? We assumed it was simply for the money. The Russian economy is brittle. But then, the question becomes, what did Iran intend with the missiles? These are not defensive weapons. And ... we can't overlook the possibility that we were meant to track these weapons to Iran. In that case, we have to consider that Russia knew what Iran intended. The endgame here is that Russia wants us to attack Iran."

"And that," said the President, "would put us into a major war." She shook her head, then looked around. "Can I get some coffee, please?" She spoke to the aide. "And see if anyone else needs anything. Let's get some sandwiches down here too. We're going to be a while."

While that was being handled, she looked to the phalanx of aides and deputies behind her. She gestured, "Zimmer?"

Janet Zimmer, a tall dark woman, stepped forward. "Yes, Madam President?"

"On the day I stepped into this job, I gave you a red leather folder and I told you to keep that with you at all times, yes?"

"Yes'm."

"Do you have it with you now?" She held out her hand.

"Yes, ma'am." Zimmer passed it over.

The President put the folder on the table in front of her. She unfastened the clasp and opened it to a page of handwritten notes. She looked around the table, waiting for silence. She didn't have to wait long. "All right. What was it John F. Kennedy said in October of 1962? Today's the day we earn our salaries." She looked to her notes and turned to the Secretary of Defense. "Secretary Garinger, I'm sure you have all the necessary scenarios, how much would a war with Iran cost?"

"Somewhere between one and three trillion dollars."

"Somewhere between one and three trillion dollars," the President repeated. "Let's assume five trillion—not just because your department always underestimates the cost of the war, but also because we're going to end up paying for all the ancillary damage to our economy as well." She picked up her pen and made a note in her folder.

"I think that's a little high, Madam President."

"Well, yes—but when has anyone brought in a war under budget?" She moved on to the next point on the page in front of her. "And how long would a war in the Mideast last?"

"Based on past experience, somewhere between three and seven years."

Let's say nine, before we could even start talking exit strategy." She added another note. "That means boys and girls who are eleven today will be in uniform before this would be over." She went on to her next note. "How many casualties among our military?"

"You need to understand, ma'am, we would be using a lot of aerial assaults to soften the target zones. We'd use drones, cruise missiles, and other remote-controlled weapons to avoid putting our own people in harm's way. But eventually, we would have to put boots on the ground. Given a prolonged conflict, we could have as many as 15,000 casualties."

"I see. 25,000, at least." The President wrote that as well."

"And how many civilian casualties?"

"Hard to say, Ma'am."

"Oh, please. We know that the last Gulf war killed 200,000 civilians. Based on that experience, we should assume at least as many civilian casualties in the next Gulf war. Probably more. Collateral damage. What a nice antiseptic term for dead children. I'll say 350,000. How does that sound?" She added that to her previous notes. "No, that's a little low. Let's make it 450,000." She crossed out her first number and wrote in the higher figure. She looked around. "I wish State were here. I'd really like her opinion, I doubt our allies will have the stomach for one more dance in the Mideast."

She started to put her pen down, then stopped herself. "Oh, one more question. What will the climate be like in the next decade? Anyone?"

Admiral Landon spoke first. "Hot. Hotter. And impossible. Might as well rename the equator. Call it the Scorch Zone. 130 degree days will be the norm in some regions."

"So all these predictions we've made about costs and casualties—? They're incomplete. Has anyone factored in the weather?"

"Well, yes—of course," said Secretary Garinger. "The weather is always part of our planning—"

"And just like all your other numbers, you're going to underestimate the severity of the situation." The President put her pen down and closed the folder. "It seems to me that Iran—all the Mideast states—are going to be dealing with some serious challenges. I don't see any compelling reason for putting our own troops in harm's way. The heat alone will be the biggest killer." She looked around the table. "No one in this room is going to be onsite. We'll be sending a generation of young men and women into hell, and the ones who survive it will come back damaged inside and out. No. Just no. We have to find a better way."

Secretary Garinger shook his head unhappily. "Madam President, with all due respect—"

"I hate that phrase," President Bourget interrupted, "because it means no respect at all."

"I apologize. I meant no insult."

"Of course not."

"What I meant to say is that we have to respond—"

"Of course, we must." The President turned around as the door of the Situation Room whooshed open. "Ahh, here's the Secretary of State. We've been waiting for you. Garinger wants to bomb Tehran. What do you think?"

"Bad idea," she said. Secretary Sharon Fetter had served as Ambassador to the United Nations before being promoted to Secretary of State. She brought a no-nonsense attitude to her negotiations, which was why she was respected, but not particularly liked.

Fetter dropped a fat notebook on the table and seated herself to the right of the President. "I've already had phone calls with Britain, France, Canada, Germany—all the usual suspects. Thoughts and prayers and so on. But—" She held up a finger as if to make a point. "They all urge caution. Everyone understands the situation, but they all made the same point. This thing could blow up very fast."

"Did anyone suggest anything useful?"

Secretary Fetter shook her head. "They're still trying to figure out how to look strong without getting any shit on their shoes. They don't want to be the next target."

Admiral Landon interrupted. "Madam President, we've identified the boat that launched the missile. We lucked out. We have satellite photos of the launch. It's heading south at top speed."

"How big a crew?" the President asked.

"Thirty-five, probably."

"Can you sink it before it gets to harbor?"

"Yes, ma'am."

"Do it."

Landon spoke to his headset. The President turned back to the Secretary of State. "Who's your best back-channel to Iran?"

"Right now? Probably Russia."

"Really?"

Secretary Fetter nodded. "Or we could go through the Swiss. They love this game."

"Go through the Swiss. Pass this message on to the Iranians. If they will deliver to the Hague, for an international war crimes tribunal, the perpetrators behind the attack on our embassy, we can avoid a prolonged and bloody war. That's the stick. The carrot? We'll unfreeze twenty-five billion dollars of their assets in our New York banks. And no patsies. We want the people who authorized the attack."

"What if they refuse?"

"They're not stupid. The president of Iran didn't order the attack. This came the extremist faction of their government. They want a war with the US. It would give them the political leverage to topple the moderates. This will give the moderates in Iran a chance to get rid of some of their worst enemies. The president will see it as an opportunity. He didn't get to be president by accident."

The Secretary of Defense interrupted. "What about our military response?"

"It's already ordered. We're sinking the ship—" The President looked across the table. "Admiral Landon? How long till confirmation?"

"Sixty seconds. The missile is in the air."

The President turned around in her chair, looking for her Chief of Staff. "Alert the networks. I'll need fifteen minutes tonight. Tell Jimmy, I'll need an expression of grief and outrage, sympathy for the families, we'll do everything necessary, etc. Gratitude for our allies who are stepping up to help, of course. Then finish up with the announcement that the ship that launched the missile is at the bottom of the Gulf. The Pentagon will hold a press conference on that tomorrow—" She looked to the head of the Joint Chiefs. "Can you manage that?"

He nodded. "Yes, Madam President."

She turned back to her Chief of Staff. "Oh, and let's put the initial blame on this splinter faction. The ones who think they're taking credit. They're a front, but let's not admit we know that. Just say that we're pursuing everyone else involved in this attack and we expect the Iranian government to cooperate with that effort. Have that on my desk in an hour. If Jimmy can type that fast. Now—"

President Bourget turned to the Secretary of State. "Send a strongly worded note to the Russian President. Be careful how you phrase it, but something to the effect that it would be dangerous for them to sell Zhukin missiles to those most likely to use them. Put it in nice diplomatic language, but make it clear that we are not happy."

Secretary Fetter nodded her agreement. "I'll have the note in front of you in an hour."

Admiral Landon pointed to the screen at the front of the room. The image was a high-definition view of a calm sea. Below, a single vessel was cutting a bright wake across the water. But only for a moment. A streak of something, a bright flash, and then a geyser of water that sent high waves rippling outward—after a moment more, except for a lingering cloud of smoke and a quick pattering of debris, the sea was calm again.

"Don't applaud," said the President, cutting off the immediate reaction. "We just killed thirty-five men. They probably had families. Wives and children. They killed for political purpose. So did we. We are not morally superior. Our hands are just as dirty. But..." She added slowly, "...what we did was necessary. Not for revenge. But to keep them from ever doing it again. And maybe, just maybe, the next people who will think to launch a missile at us will remember this and choose not to. But I wouldn't hold my breath on that either. History proves there is no shortage of idiots and assholes."

Silence returned to the Situation room.

"All right," said the President. She put her hands on the table. "Here is our official position. We mourn the loss of so many good people. Whatever public statements any of us make, always start with that. Let's focus on the tragedy, not the revenge. Yes, we have sunk the ship that launched the missile. Yes, we blame this group that claims credit. And yes, we promise to bring them to justice or bring justice to them. And yes, in the interests of world peace, we expect the cooperation of the Iranians. But we do not blame the Iranian government. We have no evidence that anyone in the Iranian government was involved. And we certainly will not mention the Russians at all. Nor will we discuss what kind of missile hit our embassy, that's for the forensics experts to determine. We are committed to taking care of the families of those who died. And we'll have—what's the protocol? A week of mourning? Flags at half-mast until the ambassador is buried? Somebody check that out, please. Is there anything I'm missing? Admiral Landon, would you please manage the room? State, you have phone calls to make. Where's my cane?" She levered herself to her feet and headed for the door. "Zimmer, bring the folder."

The President and her entourage made their way back to the Oval Office. Finally, back behind her desk, she sat down in the big leather chair, leaned her cane against the desk and sagged backward.

The California sun shone through the western windows. Bourget looked at her watch. "Are we off the clock?"

Janet Zimmer seated herself next to the desk. She nodded. "We're off the clock."

The President sighed. "Thank you. I have to tell you, that was not fun."

Zimmer said, "It's not supposed to be fun."

"How do you think I did?"

Zimmer said, "That was good. Very presidential. Better than some of the people who've played the game."

"I don't think Defense liked me."

"He's not supposed to. Everyone in government has an agenda. That was his part. But you owned the room, that was the important thing. And you didn't let anyone stampede you into a hasty decision. You weighed the political aspects against the military options. That was impressive. That red folder? Nice."

Robbie Bourget allowed herself a slight smile of satisfaction. "I think that might have been one of my better ideas. I didn't want to get so caught up in the game that I forgot who I wanted to be." She studied the cast member who played her aide. "You're a very good associate. It's hard work, isn't it?"

"Thank you, yes. We have to do a lot of behind-the-scenes preparation. It's different for every player."

"You've been doing this a long time?"

"Not as long as most. We go through a lot of cast members. It's stressful. But none of us will ever share what happens in the simulations. We're sworn to confidentiality."

Bourget nodded. "Yes, I saw that in the non-disclosure agreement. You're not allowed to release any video or evaluations. Only I can. Unfortunately, it's almost become required these days. The electorate wants to see how well a candidate can handle a crisis. I suppose it's a good idea, but I have to admit it's a little unnerving."

Zimmer said, "You should see it from our side. We never know how a candidate is going to react. It can be scary."

"You should try it from this side of the desk," said Bourget. She looked around the flawless simulation of the Oval Office. "I have to admit, it's very convincing. Too convincing."

"Thank you, yes. Backstage is a very complicated operation."

"I can imagine so."

"I assume you know the history. This happened almost by accident. Originally, this was just a standing set, rented out to anybody filming a presidential TV series or a movie. But during the last writer's strike, it became a playground for those who wanted to role-play the presidency, another cool toy for millionaires. Only a hundred thousand a day and you get a taste of the responsibilities of the office. Then during the run-up to the election year, it became a campaign stunt. Now it's a thing. Part of learning how to be a President. So, on our side, we have to take it very seriously."

Bourget nodded. "So, can I ask? What's next? Did we stop the war?"

Yes, you're allowed to ask," Zimmer said. "But if I tell you, you're not going to sleep well tonight."

"Why not?"

“Because you didn’t stop the war. Tomorrow, we go to Round Two and the whole thing blows up.”

“Huh? I don’t understand.”

“It’s a no-win situation. You’re supposed to fail.”

“But I did everything right, didn’t I? You said so. I thought—”

“Yes, you did everything right,” said Zimmer. “But that’s not the point. In here, it’s all pretend, so letting you win—that would be too easy. There’s nothing at stake. But dealing with failure—that’s the real test of any presidency. Tomorrow the simulation gets serious.”

“Are you supposed to be telling me this—?”

“Yes. Because being forewarned is also part of the job. If this were a real situation, you’d already be working on failure scenarios. So, today was just the set up. Tomorrow is the real test. What do you do when the best you can do isn’t good enough. Tomorrow is about exit strategies.”

Zimmer took a breath and stood up. “Madam President, this is the reason we have a non-disclosure policy. Because now that you know what kind of crap you might have to deal with if you get elected—and what failure looks like when your best isn’t enough, maybe you’ll understand just how hard you have to work to keep these messes from happening in the first place.” She offered her hand. “Good luck to you, Ma’am. I’ll see you tomorrow morning.”

Basic Training

Alison McBain

Five weeks ago.

It hadn't been sudden or unexpected. It hadn't been a surprise. Despite that, Adrianne found herself looking for her girlfriend Samantha at the grocery store or in the line at the ATM. As she drove past a bus stop, the teen waiting there turned her head, and Adrianne almost stopped the car in seeing a familiar tilt of chin. But the chin wasn't attached to the right face—the only face she craved to see.

When Adrianne got home, she got out a blank sheet of paper and pen, but stopped after writing, "Dear Sam."

She didn't know what to say, not to a piece of paper. She left it lying on the kitchen table with just the two words on it, the pen crosswise against them, like a knife cutting the words in half.

Seven weeks ago.

"You can't go." Adrianne's hands were scrubbing the same spot over and over on an already-clean dish, but her eyes focused on Sam.

Sam was sitting at the kitchen table, her booted feet kicked out in front of her, hands crossed over her stomach. Although Adrianne knew it was deliberate, an act of nonchalance, it still pissed the hell out of her. There was fear beneath Sam's calm, there had to be. The images of sand and camouflage and guns were so frequently on the news that one could claim desensitization, unless being sent right into it.

But when Sam didn't move or respond, Adrianne threw the plate she was washing into the sink. It broke with a dull thunk.

Sam dropped her eyes to Adrianne's stilled hands. Told her, "Stop being dramatic."

"Why should I stop?"

"It's not like you."

Adrianne's eyes were wet, but she ignored the moisture. "Oh, I'm sorry! Like the decision is irrevocable. You don't have to go." Adrianne always pulled out the "dictionary words" when she wanted to annoy, knew it made Sam feel small.

Hiccups rose up in Adrianne's throat, and she took a step away from the sink, not knowing what to do next.

Sam frowned, then stood, but didn't move closer. "Don't, Addy."

"I can't... I can't..." She pressed her lips together as her throat closed. Regardless, the words escaped into the air, unsaid. Sam turned away and walked out of the room.

As Adrianne moved back to the sink to pick up the pieces of the broken plate, she felt like the shit she was. She doubted her mother would notice one missing dish. Her brother took out the trash, and he was about as observant as a bulldozer, so he would never tell. Still, she wanted to take all those pieces and glue them back together, to make something whole out of what she had wrecked. To go back in time.

The front door closed quietly as she dumped the pieces into the trash. Sam never made a fuss, not like her. But Adrianne could still hear the loud crash of the unslammed door over the splash of running water.

<<>>

They wasted three days. Three precious days out of those last two weeks left to them, before Adrianne swallowed her pride and called. Sam had outwaited her, as always.

"I'm sorry," Adrianne forced out the familiar words. It seemed like she was always apologizing. It didn't help knowing that she was often wrong—she was the hotheaded one, the one to blow her cool over an imagined insult. It didn't help that this time, the insult wasn't so imagined. "I'm sorry about the fight. I should have listened to you without getting mad. But I just don't see why—"

"Addy!" Sam's voice was sharp.

"Okay. I won't say it." She heard the pique in her own voice, and suddenly laughed at herself for how childish she sounded. It was hard to hold a grudge against Sam, even if she tried.

She could hear the answering smile in Sam's voice. "My parents are gone."

"Okay."

"Come over."

It was always like this. They fought—or, rather, Adrianne fought, like a single racquetball player bouncing the ball against a wall. But when they came together, there was no disagreement. There were lips and warm skin, the supple twining together of limbs, hands, teeth, tongue.

Afterwards, Adrianne stroked a palm down Sam's cheek, following the concave hollow of neck to collarbone. She felt the pressure of her lover, the regard like a weight. But when Adrianne glanced at her, Sam looked away.

"Two months," Sam said. She wound a strand of Adrianne's blonde hair around one finger and let it spring back. Her eyes followed the hair rather than meet Adrianne's gaze. "I'll see you again, after Basic."

"And then you won't. You'll be deployed right afterwards."

"Write me a letter or an email once in a while." Sam finally looked up, grinning. "Blondes *do* know how to write, don't they?"

Adrianne laughed helplessly. "Bitch."

"Skank."

More laughter, over the hollow feeling. The center of her had been missing ever since Sam told her she planned to enlist after their high school graduation.

Ten weeks ago.

"You're kidding, right?"

For once, Sam wouldn't meet her eyes head-on. Shrugged.

"But your brothers have done it. Your parents don't expect *you*—"

Eyes hardened and moved back to Adrianne, front and center. "Why not *me*?"

"You're a g—"

"If you say girl," Sam interrupted. "I will whup your white ass from here back to where it came from."

That shut her up. It always did. "But Sam—"

"But nothing. I've told you because you deserve to know. This isn't opinion. This is fact."

So Adrianne had shut up. She had believed Sam when she said it was too late to change her mind.

<<>>

But maybe it hadn't been too late—then.

Now, it certainly was.

That last week and a half flew by, and it was suddenly D-day—the day before departure. The army was still catching up with providing adequate co-ed training facilities, so women training for combat weren't just living in the next town—they were moving halfway across the country. The bus left the next morning, early.

"Write."

"Yes," Adrianne said.

"I love you."

"Yes," Adrianne said.

Sam hugged her, hard. The angles of her face had changed. They were foreign to Adrianne, a map of a different place. A different time.

"When's the bus?" she asked.

Sam pulled back. Wound a strand of Adrianne's blonde hair around her finger and let it slowly slide off again. "I'm sorry," Sam said finally, not looking away from the curl of yellow hair she was playing with. "You probably shouldn't come tomorrow."

The words were like a punch in the gut. Sam was not furtive in hiding the two of them from her family, but there were some things they didn't talk about with their parents right now. Perhaps not ever.

"Okay," Adrianne said instead, like the inevitable tick of the clock. They hadn't touched, *really* touched, since making up after the last fight, and she knew what Sam's hug had been for. Adrianne wanted to be brave, like a military wife, but it was proving an effort to even smile.

"Okay." Sam seemed distracted. So Adrianne just stood there like a lump and watched as Sam walked down the driveway and turned left at the sidewalk to go home. Sam looked back at the last moment—looked back and waved. Then she was gone, and Adrianne went back inside.

The next day, she heard Sam laughing at the grocery store. She saw Sam walking down the street. Sam's favorite song was on her shuffle play. When she walked by an electronics store, soldiers hunkered down on the many TVs, surrounded by grit and dust. They all had Sam's face.

When Adrianne went home, she took out a pen and paper and wrote "Dear Sam" in black, indelible ink. She couldn't manage anything else, so she went to bed. Her pillow smelled like Sam's shampoo.

She went for a walk in the park and saw Sam at the water fountain. Running around the track. Riding a bicycle. Adrianne went home and wrote: "Dear Sam." Her eyes were dry as bone when she went to bed.

Her cell rang in the morning from the kitchen table, where she'd left it the night before. "Addy," her mother called to her in Sam's voice. She dragged herself out of bed to pick up the phone, and it was Sam speaking.

Only it wasn't.

After two weeks, she was thrown into a paroxysm of guilt. She bought a new ream of paper and tried harder. "Dear Sam," she wrote. "Dear Sam, Dear Sam, Dear Sam..."

The letters disconnected from the page and became meaningless, floating through the air like dragonflies. She went back to bed.

Adrianne's mother noticed in the third week. She talked at her daughter, asking stupid questions and not listening to the half-hearted replies. "Go away," she finally told her mom. Her mother went. Friends from high school stopped by. Even her brother tried, but only in the bored way of a teenager, too cool to really care.

She didn't know what day it was when there was a quiet knock on her bedroom door, and Sam's voice said, "Adrianne."

She sat up, startled. Only it wasn't Sam—the voice was similar, but older.

A woman came into the room, outlined by light from the hall. It wasn't until she sat on the bed that Adrianne saw that it was Glenda, Sam's mother.

She was shocked, as if a ghost had returned after an exorcism. Adrianne braced herself for a motherly lecture, but Glenda said nothing for several moments.

Adrianne studied her, seeing her as if for the first time. Glenda's hair had streaks of white in it and was pulled back tightly from her scalp in a thick braid down her back. She smelled familiar, like Sam's lavender soap, but she looked tired. "I know you miss her," Glenda finally said.

The statement was so absurd that Adrianne laughed. Realizing how rude that would seem, she said, "Yes." But she couldn't think of what else to say. Glenda's eyes were soft, like her daughter's.

"I miss her, too," Glenda said. "A mother's love is special—just like other types of love can be. Even though she has her own way to walk, it doesn't mean love needs to stop."

"Right." The anger leaked into Adrianne's voice, she knew it did, and she couldn't seem to stop it. "But she didn't do it for herself. She did it for you—so she wouldn't be left out. How will you live with yourself if she doesn't come back?"

Just like when Adrianne argued with Sam, the angry words bounced off Glenda with little impression. "Love can stop," Sam's mother told her. "Or it can go on." With that, she put her hand on Adrianne's bright blonde hair, a brief touch. "She misses you," she said gravely before getting up and walking out.

Adrianne lay back in her unwashed sheets and stared at the dark ceiling. There was a lamp on in the hall, and Glenda had left the door open. The light seeped into her room, creating shadows. Almost, she could see Sam's face in the twilight.

Almost.

The next day, she got up and showered. Washed her sheets, cleaned her room, and recycled the mess of papers with only two words on them.

In her desk drawer, she found a pair of scissors. She weighed them in her palm, considering, then wound a strand of her hair around one finger. A quick snick of the scissors, and she let the cut strand of blonde hair drip off her hand and into an envelope.

A week later, her mom handed her the mail, and she saw the letter on top addressed to her. She took it into her room and sat on her bed in the dark. With both hands, Adrianne held the unopened envelope against her face.

And she cried and she cried and she cried.

The Mirror Fields

Rob Francis

We live in the Shara and are fortunate to do so. That's what Kimal says when he brings supplies to my sun orchard. "Another fine day in the Shara, Bol, my lucky lamb. And work to be done!"

Kimal's a good shepherd. One of the best. Never stays long but always unloads the boxes of rice, nuts and dried fruit from the old jeep and helps me pack them in my little shelter before he fills up my water tank from the big tank on the jeep and adds the chlorine tablets. It doesn't take him long: he's much bigger and stronger than me. We talk as we put the food away, and I tell Kimal I wish I was more like him, so that one day I could be a shepherd and drive a jeep and go fight in the war. Even if I don't mean it. Not really. I just don't want to disappoint him. Mostly I want the war to end, so my life can begin.

He says I'll be like him one day. I'll grow tough on all this food and work, and by the end of the war I'll be a great man and ready to be a shepherd in turn, should the Sunrisers raise their ugly heads again after our victory, which must surely come soon. "The harder the work, the harder the man!" That's another one of Kimal's sayings.

He doesn't tell me much about the war. I guess it's because he doesn't want to worry me. As I say, Kimal's a good shepherd.

We've been at war with the Sunrisers for as long as I can remember. I don't know when it started. Maybe there was peace, back when I was just a little kid at the stable. But by the time I was sent to the orchard, the war was on. Kimal always says we're winning, though I'm not sure why it's taking so long. If I ask, he just grins and says something clever, like, "Do as I ask and stick to your task!" Or, "Hold your line and all will be fine! We've all got to work hard to make sure we win."

Once the supplies are packed away, Kimal takes the charged batteries out of the great concrete store, replaces them with dead ones, loads up the jeep, and is off to the next orchard, barking out "Work to be done," through the gap where the jeep's door should be, waving and smiling as he goes.

I usually watch until he's gone before picking up my brush and cloth and resuming my work, which is cleaning the dust off the flat, wide panels of the sun trees, then polishing them until they glisten with their peculiar deep blackness. I'm not sure why they're called trees. I've never seen a real tree, which the teachers at the stable told me are made of wood and have hundreds of green or brown leaves all over them. A sun tree is nothing like that, though perhaps the shape is the same. Each one has a central pole and frame covered by a dome of interlocking sheets to catch the sun from all directions. I can just about reach the top panels with my stepladder. There are two hundred and thirty trees on my orchard, each with a dozen panels, and the work is never-ending. There's so much dust in the Shara that as soon as I've finished, it's time to start again. In the summer I wake when it's dark and I clean and polish until it's too hot to bear, then I eat and sleep, and then I start again. In the winter, I do my best to stay warm during the night and sweep all through the day. Every three or four days, Kimal arrives with supplies.

It's not so bad, I guess. But the war will end one day and when I leave the orchard behind, I won't look back.

<<>>

I conduct my cleaning carefully. I always begin in the southwest corner of the orchard and count to a thousand as I dust and polish each tree before moving onto the next one. Doing this means that sometimes—perhaps once every four or five days—I arrive at the wire fence that marks the orchard's eastern boundary at the same time as Mishra reaches it from her side. She's the only other sweeper I've ever seen. I don't know who sweeps the orchards to the north, west or south of mine. Our paths have never crossed. But Mishra is the only other sweeper I need to see.

She's a little older than me, though we're about the same height. At every meeting we stand facing each other through the fence and I take time to make sure I see her clearly. Her eyes are deep, and dark, and kind. She leans on her broom casually, head cocked to the side, listening to what I have to say about the day. Then she tells me about her trees, what she's been eating, what animals she might've seen or heard. She asks how I am, how I feel. What I've been dreaming about. What I think tomorrow will be like.

We don't talk about the war, or Kimal. Mishra frowns if I mention them. Instead, we pretend we are the only people in the entire Shara. Sometimes I wish we were.

We usually talk a little about growing up in our stables. They were largely the same, at least as far as I can tell from Mishra's stories. A handful of shepherds and shepherdesses looking after all the lambs, getting us ready to serve. Teaching us to read and write, but also to work the land, to make things, fix things. Sometimes to fight, but those lessons were not for everyone. I never learned those sorts of things. Neither did Mishra, I guess.

Sometimes I pull down the strip of cloth I use to cover my mouth and nose from the endless dust and press my lips to the wire. She touches mine with hers, just lightly; and we curl our fingers through the mesh so that they fold over each other, almost as if we are holding hands. In these moments I forget everything else.

Her hair carries the scent of thyme. She says there is a patch of it in her orchard and sometimes she crushes the leaves and runs the oil through her dark curls. I catch its perfume in my dreams.

It is never for long; there is always so much work to do. The dust is never-ending. But Mishra is always there again a few days later.

Waiting for me. Waiting for the war to end.

<<>>

One evening in spring, a sandstorm comes, the worst I've ever seen. The sky is blind, the sun trees drenched in dust. Sweeping is impossible. I sit in my shelter to wait it out, sleeping some and dreaming of Mishra. Imagining what we might do after the war, if she chooses the same path as me, or I her. Whatever it might be.

I am dozing when I hear it: a low growl overhead that quickly grows into an unhinged scream. I race outside, the cloth over my face. The noise is as if the Shara itself is tearing apart, surely the loudest sound that's ever been heard. For a moment the sky darkens even more, and then it passes and the screaming fades.

I return to my shelter.

The sand-blizzard lasts long into the night, but I can no longer sleep. I'm wide awake when the stranger pushes open the door and stumbles inside.

He is the desert itself; there's no part of him not smothered in ochre dust. He's tall, as tall as Kimal, though not as broad. A backpack is strapped across his shoulders, and after a moment I realise he wears a mask to cover his mouth and nose; a curled pipe leads from it to the pack.

He looks about the shelter; at me, the boxes of food, my pallet on the floor, the small wind-up lamp that dimly illuminates the confined space. He tugs the mask off, revealing thin lips and a small beard. He frowns, then sits on the floor, legs crossed, and bows his head for a moment as if exhausted.

"Water," he says, still looking at the floor. He pronounces the word slowly and strangely.

"What?" I say, though I heard him clearly. My voice catches.

"Wa-water, please."

I take my cup and fill it from the tank, set it down before him. As he moves to pick it up, a small pistol shifts at his waist, a band of red tape across the grip.

He drinks, emptying the cup, and looks at me carefully.

"Children," he says in his odd accent, as if to himself. "All children."

I stand taller. "I'm almost a man."

He smiles.

"You keep the..." He says a word I don't understand, then frowns and shakes his head, begins rooting for something in his dust-covered jacket.

"The sun trees? Yes. That's my job. Mine alone."

He nods.

"Thank you." He places the cup on the floor once more, an equal distance between us.

"You're a Sunriser, aren't you?" I should be afraid, but I'm not.

He nods again and pulls a small grey disc from his jacket pocket.

"Are you going to kill me?"

He taps the disc a few times and speaks into it, in another language. A moment later a smooth female voice projects from the disc.

"I do not harm children."

He smiles sadly.

"Why are you here?"

The disc relays his words. "Scouting. Looking. This is a battery farm?"

"Battery...? Yes. I suppose so. The trees power the batteries, and they get taken away. I don't know what for."

"Lots of things," says the disc. "Barracks, houses, prisons. Trains. But mainly weapons."

He points to the ceiling. "The desert has the sun. So much energy, over such a large area. But capturing it..." He opens his arms. "You have a fine farm here." He stands. "Thank you for the water. I must go now."

The man reaches into a pocket and draws forth a long strip of red cloth with angular black symbols across it that I don't recognise. He holds it out and, after a few moments of indecision, I take it. The fabric is wonderfully smooth, so that I cannot help running it through my fingers as I examine the symbols minutely.

"When the time comes, wear this. It will help to keep you safe. And go east. East! North, and you will die, or remain a slave. South, there is only more war. And west, there is only the endless desert, once you pass beyond the battery farms. Safety is in the east. Remember that! Don't worry, young man: you'll be free soon."

"Free to do what?" I say, but when I look up the stranger has gone. I cross to the door and peer out. There is only the red dust, choking the world.

<<>>

The storm has passed by morning. I step out into a landscape remade, drifts of sand piled against the sun trees, their great flat sheets thickly layered with dust. I need to start sweeping, but before that I must check on Mishra—at least as far as I can.

I make my way to the eastern fence, stepping through the new dunes that stretch about me in sweeping curves.

My heart lifts to see her waiting there, her hair grey with dust so that she looks deceptively old, her eyes half-closed with tiredness.

We clasp our fingers together through the wire.

She smiles. "Quite the storm last night."

"You're okay?"

She nods. "Did you hear—something, a noise, like the sky breaking?"

"I did. And there was..."

"What?"

I'm not sure whether to mention the stranger, even to Mishra, but just then a rumbling announces the arrival of Kimal's jeep, rolling along my side of the eastern fence, over the humps of sand.

Before it even arrives, Mishra squeezes my fingers and lets go, walking away into her orchard.

Kimal drops down from the jeep and grins.

"Bol! Glad to see you're well after such a night. A tough lamb indeed! And a good job you're already out working, with so much to do. Hard work makes a hard man, remember."

He stares off into Mishra's orchard, and I follow his gaze. I catch a glimpse Mishra's hair before it moves behind one of the trees, and I wonder if she's watching us both.

I lift my brush a little to show I'm prepared. "Yes, Kimal. I'm ready to start sweeping."

Kimal steps forward and puts his hand on my shoulder, squeezing it hard for a moment so that the muscles spasm and I almost wince.

"An uneventful night for you, Bol? Did you hear anything unusual? See anything strange?"

I nod. "There was a great noise from the sky for a little while, but it passed."

"I see." There is a long silence while Kimal looks at the bright blue sky as if whatever caused that terrible cacophony might still be there. Then he looks me in the eye.

"And you didn't see anyone? No-one came through your orchard? None of the other sweepers, or... any strangers?"

I swallow. I should tell the truth about the Sunriser, of course. But I can't. I'm not sure why. Perhaps I'm afraid Kimal will be disappointed that I didn't fight him. Perhaps something else. The red fabric is still carefully folded in the pocket of my trousers.

"No. After I heard the noise I went to sleep. By the time I woke the storm was almost over."

"Right. Good!" He stares into Mishra's orchard again for moment, his face blank. His hand slips off my shoulder.

Seconds later he's back in the jeep, hands turning the wheel, calling to me once more as the jeep pulls away.

"Another fine day in the Shara, Bol, and work to be done!"

I turn to the nearest tree and begin sweeping.

<<>>

Three nights later I'm woken by the rumble of the jeep. I peer out of my shelter into the black desert, knowing that something must be wrong. Kimal never visits at night. The jeep is dark in the moonlight as it rolls to a stop in front of me. The lights are off. The handbrake crunches and Kimal jumps down.

"Kimal?"

He says nothing at first but goes to the back of the jeep and pulls out a sledgehammer, which he tosses at my feet.

"The Sunrisers are coming, Bol. Coming fast. The most important thing now is to make sure they can't use the orchards. Take this hammer and smash the trees, quick as you can."

He pulls a gun from his belt; a small grey pistol with red tape across the grip. He hands it to me.

"There are two bullets in there, Bol." Kimal holds up two fingers to emphasise his point. "One should be enough, but there's another, in case the first one isn't... clean. You understand what I'm saying?"

I nod.

"You don't want them to catch you, Bol. Believe me. But smash the trees first. All of them."

He climbs back into the jeep.

"Where are you going, Kimal?"

"To the next orchard. I have a lot of lambs, and they all need to be warned. Work to be done." The jeep swings around and rolls away. Kimal extends a hand in farewell.

I watch the jeep disappear into the night.

I leave the hammer on the ground. The Sunrisers are the enemy, but they are not *my* enemy. I've spent years tending to my orchard, ever since the stable sent me here. I'm not going to smash the trees now.

Besides, if the Sunrisers *are* coming, Mishra may be in danger.

Holding the gun tight I run north, towards the orchard gate. The sun trees loom on either side of me, already dusty in the moonlight, needing to be swept.

The gate is open. Kimal has driven through and not stopped to close and lock it, and for the first time in years I pass beyond the limits of my orchard.

A well-driven path stretches along endless rows of high wire fence, the sun orchards extending as far as I can see.

An incandescent flash lights up the sky far to the north and for a moment all of the sun trees blaze like mirrors, field after field of them.

I turn east and run to the gate to Mishra's orchard. It too is open.

Chest heaving, lungs burning, I race along the rows of sun trees to where I know Mishra's shelter must stand, in the same place mine does. As I get close, the idling rumble of Kimal's jeep comes to me on the breeze.

I stop.

Kimal has his hand on Mishra's arm, she is pulling away, but he's holding so tight she can't break free. They are both snarling at each other.

“Girl, get in the car! You don’t want to be here when the Sunrisers arrive. You don’t know what they’ll do to you.”

“I know what’ll happen if I get in that car with *you*. Leave me here. Now!”

I’m not sure what’s happening, but I know enough that whatever the problem is, Mishra must be right. Kimal’s a good shepherd but Mishra is Mishra.

I step forward without thinking, the gun raised and pointed at Kimal.

“Mishra, are you okay?”

Kimal twists and looks at me silently, intently, like a snake about to strike. Mishra continues to struggle but Kimal is too strong. There’s another gun at his waist, tucked into his belt. A silver handgun of a type I’ve seen before, in the hands of shepherds at my stable.

“That gun was a gift, Bol.” Kimal talks quietly, almost as if to himself. “Two bullets, remember. If you use them on me, what will you do when the enemy come? They’ll hurt you bad, Bol.”

My hand wavers a little as I try to keep the gun levelled at Kimal and away from Mishra.

“Please, Kimal. Let Mishra go. She needs to smash her sun trees, too. Doesn’t she?”

“And two bullets won’t be enough, Bol,” he says, as if he hasn’t even heard me. “You’ve never used a gun, so you don’t know. But you know me. How strong I am. Two bullets won’t even hurt me, Bol. Two bullets is only enough for you.”

He’s right. Kimal’s the biggest and strongest shepherd I’ve ever seen. Two bullets wouldn’t be enough. I lower the gun and he nods in satisfaction.

“Good lamb. Now, go smash your trees.”

He turns away, still holding onto Mishra’s arm, but she is quick as a scorpion as she snatches the gun from Kimal’s belt. Two shots ring loud on the night air. Kimal grunts and falls hard. He groans, gives a little sigh, and is still.

I stare at Mishra, at the gun in her hand. And the one in mine.

“Mishra!”

“Come on,” she says, grabbing my hand— properly, for the first time—and pulling me to the jeep, with its big water tank and food for resupplying the farms. We climb in and she puts her gun in the bin between the seats. The sky lights up once more, and this time there is the faint boom of thunder. Or something else.

"That's not a storm, is it?" I try to keep the fear from my voice but it pushes through anyway.

Mishra shoves the gear stick around and grabs the wheel. "No. It isn't."

"You can drive?"

"I learnt in my stable."

The jeep lurches forward, shaking, and then moves more smoothly, bouncing just a little over the dry ground. We pass along the sun trees and out of the gate, onto the long track that stretches east and west, running forever through the sun orchards.

"Which way?" Mishra raises her eyebrows. I'm sure she's already decided, but she wants to know what I think.

"West," I say. "I vote for west. The desert and the darkness."

She nods and turns the jeep away from the lightening horizon.

"They're coming, aren't they?" I ask the question more to myself than to Mishra, but still she answers.

"Yes."

"Do you think they'll kill us?"

"Maybe. Maybe not. Why would they? Why wouldn't they?"

She wipes her face, one hand on the steering wheel, as the jeep picks up speed. The wind blows dust and sand through the spaces where the doors should be. It stings my skin.

I still have the gun in my hand, the red tape across the grip dark with sweat.

I pull the red fabric from my pocket and examine it once more as the sky flickers. I consider tying it round my arm or head. But should I? Maybe I'm already free. Maybe wearing this would mark me as a lamb again, for a different shepherd. I hesitate.

Then Mishra tugs a strip from her own pocket—the same bright red, the same black symbols—and lets the wind play with it, one hand on the wheel, the other waving the fabric so that it trails across my face. I laugh.

After a few moments we both let go, so that the slivers of fabric are torn away by the wind, disappearing into the night.

I turn to look at Mishra, to make sure I see her clearly. Her silhouette is deep and dark and beautiful.

"Where are we going?"

"Does it matter?"

Dawn is breaking behind us, another long and dusty day in the Shara. The flashes and thunder are closer now, but I'm not so scared anymore. Mishra is here. Mishra will always be here.

I put my gun next to hers between the seats.

"No," I say. "It doesn't." It is the truth, and it is enough.

We drive, trying to outrun the daylight. Together.

The Song of Telemakhos

Peter Tacy

When I was younger
I thought it was *my* story, of
how my days of longing
ended. How I'd stood
aft, where I'd seen my father
standing as he sailed away…

Of how I found him
and how my powerlessness
to defend home, kin,
and mother from debauchery
ended—as we two, now one,
father and reclaimed son,
slew them. We killed them all. We
cleansed our home with blood—
washed the floors, tables,
long dining benches and
even the limestone walls
with blood. Their blood.

But that is his story.

The years passed.
I learned to rule. I learned
how unforgiving grief can be,
even if the grief is for the unforgivable.
I found that lives protected

and love requited matter more
than any man's adventure. I learned
the hardness of hatred
and the legacy of vengeance. And
I learned about the cost of true justice.
You see, having grown up fatherless,
without a ruler to emulate,
I learned ruling
On the job.

Those lessons saved me. They saved
my sons, my daughters, my wife,
and my people. But they were
bitter lessons. They led me to a
bitter fate...to forever lie
outside *the story*; to be son
of a canny voyager who wrecked
monsters and shipmates equally;
a mere footnote to *his* epic.

But now—now I know the truth
is indeed mine, and not my father's.
Yet how can it be *the story?*

Within my walls
my grandsons read of *him*, not me.
They live in peace, but study war,
learn that leaving home on a fool's errand,
summoned by another man's vengeance
is *grand*, virtuous, even sane; that
abandoning the loved to survive or perish
as heartlessly as the capricious gods
abandoned blameless Andromache—
heiress to a throne, or a slave and concubine—
either—at a toss—as a
mere token in a game of men and gods—
is the mark of a man we call a hero.

Chancing us to such a fate, my father set forth.
And yes, a great singer set his story,
not mine.

My lesson is here.
But who will teach it? Who will sing it?

A small heroism begets a small poetry.

Reaping the Iron Harvest, Again...

Ann Poore

And we will reap what we have sown-
An iron harvest yields bitter crops...

In fertile ground we plant our sons,
In the bloody rain they flourish.
But before they're grown,
They are scythed down,
For the iron harvest.

The sound of bugles clearly call,
And sons and daughters
Proudly answer-
Ripe for slaughter
In the iron harvest.

And so we fight and still they die.
From world to world and back again,
Our children are
Ploughed under,
For the iron harvest.

Then cradled in the mouldy bones
Of long dead brothers,
Their ghosts sing songs of bygone days-
Laments of pain
From the iron harvest.

But soon enough the land lies fallow,
Rich and ready for hurt and harrow,
Waiting for the bitter rain
Of tears and blood,
And the iron harvest.

And as years pass in grief and pain,
The seeds of strife we plant again,
And flesh and bone
Are flensed and crushed,
For the iron harvest.

And so we reap what we have sown-
The iron harvest of our sons and daughters...

The High Road

Gustavo Bondoni

Karina shaded her eyes against the sun which rose pale over the peak, casting elongated shadows over the ground. She could hear the bubbling of the water heating on her camp stove.

"It is fixed, the last one." Ernesto's breath hung in the morning air.

"Just in time." She poured boiling water over the precious coca leaves, now in short supply. They'd each earned a cup after the night's major milestone.

The infusion sharpened her senses and she heard Juana's sharp clicking gait coming up the path, a bit envious of Ernesto's grandmother's ability to go up and down the hill ten times a day. She herself had stayed on the mountain with Ernesto, each sleeping under a blanket. The path wasn't easy for her, and they had worked through the night.

Juana arrived, not even breathing hard. "Is it done?"

He nodded. "It's done."

"I knew you wouldn't fail us." She smiled. "We're almost out of coca!"

"You had more confidence than I did."

Fourteen drones, ancient, battered, and scratched, lay in a row along the path. The one Ernesto had spent the night rewiring sat proudly with the rest. The machines were a mix of civilian and military equipment, all of the medium- to heavy-lift helicopter persuasion. Fixed-wing drones were useless for the task.

"Where is your hat, chica?" Juana scolded her. "You will fry in the sun."

"It's just dawn. I'll be fine." Still, she put on the hat.

Unlike Ernesto and Juana, who sported the dark, greyish skin and razor-thin physiques of the mountain folk, Karina was blonde and round-faced, albeit no longer the chubby tourist she'd been when the war had trapped her in Peru. Constant climbing had turned fat into muscle.

"I brought some food," Juana said, unwrapping a cloth bundle from which she pulled maize pancakes and a thermos. The last item she removed was a syringe, which she handed to Karina.

Karina lifted her shirt to expose her stomach and injected herself. She saw Ernesto and Juana exchange looks. Everyone knew she had very little insulin left. When she ran out…

Karina fought down the panic. That, not the coca, was the reason their project was so urgent.

It had been a risk to take the Camino Inca with diabetes, but she'd arranged to restock at various spots along the way, and carried a small rechargeable cooler that held a week's supply.

She hadn't counted on the war closing the trail, stranding her on a mountain away from her next supply of insulin. The only reason she was still alive was that this village had been one of her original drop points, with backup power generation. She'd had plenty of insulin brought in for the road ahead, but with the unexpected conflict, she was down to her last few vials.

"Are you sure the drones can lift the rope?" Juana looked doubtful.

Karina nodded. "Barely. And we need to pray that the wind will stay down. But if conditions help us… yeah, we should be fine."

Even after eight months in Peru, Karina knew her Spanish still sounded like that of a Brazilian tourist. One of thousands who'd been on the Camino Inca when the war came, but the only one who'd been stranded in their isolated village.

"When will you start?"

She popped the last of the pancake in her mouth. "Now. Before the wind comes up."

Ernesto nodded and returned to the old stone hut. His voice drifted out to them as he shouted into the old radio.

"Pablo, can you hear me?"

"Hi Ernesto, you're up early." The volume of the reply was clearly turned up all the way.

"I wish. I'm up late. We're flying the rope over in a few minutes."

A long silence ensued. "Really? I can't believe you managed it."

"Really. Have you set up the anchor point?"

Karina waited tensely for the reply, wishing she was the one speaking to the people who could save her life, but they could afford no miscommunication, and her Spanish was not quite up to it.

"We did. But to be honest, we weren't expecting to have to use it."

"Heh. This Brazilian woman is really something. She wants to live forever."

"Well, if she pulls this off, she just might."

Ernesto emerged as Karina and Juana were clipping the last of the drones to the jury-rigged harness that would keep the drones all stable in relation to each other. Then, reverently, Karina pulled an old radio control device from her backpack, the only suitable instrument she'd located in the village.

Pablo's mountain was only a few hundred meters away, but it might have been on the moon. The roads between the two settlements had been blasted to pieces and mined. Automated gun emplacements in the valley were still operational, powered by more of the microhydroelectric plants common in the area, shooting at anything that got too close without the correct passcodes. They'd been designed to stop armored columns, which meant that civilians who walked too close were turned into hamburger. That's what happened to the guides and other hikers who had been with Karina. No one knew how to remove the guns, the automation showed no signs of switching itself off, and she couldn't afford to wait until they ran out of ammo.

So most villages survived on what they had in hand, what they could grow on the tiny plots of land in their gardens, the way it had been before the advent of modern civilization.

Of course, Karina thought fondly, as she watched Juana adjust a rope, most villages didn't have a steel-willed village elder like

Juana. She'd pulled everyone in the village together and made them inventory what they had. Essentially, the brief advent of war had left them with the food they could grow, not enough coca, large quantities of drones and miles of cable. That, some welders, an electronics technician and a Brazilian programmer who happened to be trapped there with them decided the course of action.

Each of the drones powered up smoothly, until the very last one, which blinked on and then, abruptly shut off. Her heart sank as she contemplated that she might die because of one drone.

"Hand me the screwdriver," Ernesto said. "Hurry. I need to get this fixed while the others are still working." He opened the hatch and, to her relief, she saw the problem immediately. A lead had come undone, probably jostled loose by the trip up the mountain.

"There, the green wire, see it?"

"Thanks." Ernesto pressed it in and within minutes, all the drones were floating five meters off the ground.

"So far so good." She could feel a trickle of sweat run down her face despite the cool mountain air.

"Will they hold the weight?"

"If my calculations are correct… yeah. If not, just fix whatever breaks and try again. You don't need me. The theory is sound."

Ernesto didn't answer, but Karina could see the shock written in his expression. She'd been contemplating death for months… and an unpleasant death at that. She'd made her peace, to a degree.

But that didn't mean she wouldn't fight like hell to stay alive.

Ernesto hooked the end of a rope to the harness and Karina directed the drone formation towards the peak across the valley, barely visible in the mist.

The drones lifted a length of rope into the air and Karina's hopes lifted with it, but not too high: the problem wasn't lifting a little rope a few meters; it was pulling enough rope to cross the gap between peaks without letting it slacken so much that the middle would get into the crosshairs of the murder machines below.

That was why they needed all fourteen drones.

Karina watched them pull, felt each gust of wind as if it was the end of the world, and held her breath when the drone formation disappeared from sight in a cloud.

"Pull the ropes back," she ordered.

Ernesto tugged on the winch until the drone formation came back into view like a kite on a string, and then they all waited tensely for the accumulated mist to disperse. When it looked like it wasn't going to happen, Karina said: "I think I see the mountain ahead," and drove them back into the cloud bank. "Damn, this was so much easier back when these things had cameras and GPS. Ernesto, can you call them and ask if they see us?"

Ernesto manned the radio. "Pablo, can you see the drones?"

"Yes! You need to come down a few meters. And move to the right."

"Our right or yours?"

This way, by careful increments and with breath held against the knowledge that a sharp gust of wind would shatter her dreams against the mountainside, she brought the drones towards the waiting arms of the people of the nearest village, men and women who lived less than an hour's walk away—once you figured the walking down the hills and back up—but whom they hadn't seen in months.

"We've threaded the rope into our winch," Pablo told them.

"Pull."

The rope became fully taut and the winch on their side of the divide began to turn. Soon, the splice where cable replaced rope came through the winch and began to cross the gap. That join was the most reinforced part of the line, but it was also the weakest link. If the weight of the cable was too much, that was where it would break.

All she could do was to hope it held.

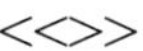

The cage was stronger than it needed to be, but Juana's welding crew had heard people would be riding through the sky in it and decided that sturdy was the way to go.

Karina had criticized the time it took and the extra weight, but she was thankful now.

Ernesto had gone first, pulling himself along hand over hand. The nearest of the cage's wheels—old pulley wheels—squeaked as it rolled along the wire.

Minutes later, it was her turn. The valley below, green trees and grey rock, was so far beneath her that a fall would turn her to jelly. She wondered if the killing machines would track her as she dropped. She might be dead of gunfire before she hit the ground.

The cage swayed in every gust of wind, causing Karina's stomach to jump around. Unlike her friends, she hadn't been born miles up in the mountains.

An eternity later, she arrived at the other side of the valley. "This is Karina." Ernesto pulled her from the cage. "She was the one flying the drones."

Pablo shook hands with her. "Thanks for helping us link our towns together again. You have no idea what it means to us."

Karina held back, shy. She'd felt the same way with the villagers when they realized they were trapped. It had taken several days before she dared speak to anyone, and that was Juana, who'd apparently decided she would make Karina talk. When Juana decided something would happen, it happened.

Karina'd been lucky that Juana had done so.

"Where's the pharmacy?" Ernesto said.

"In the village, over here." Pablo gestured at what was left of their town.

Karina was shocked.

This had once been a settlement of several dozen houses, but most of them were rubble now, with a few flickering lights to show that some of its power-generation capability had survived. Unlike Ernesto's own, nameless village, the fighting hadn't passed this place by. Concepción had been hammered by both sides… even though the villagers never even knew who was fighting or what the war was about.

They walked in silence. The pharmacy door was open and the lights were on inside. That was a relief, and it made sense: some of the medicine within—including insulin—had probably needed to be refrigerated. Karina rushed in, while Ernesto and Pablo talked outside.

"What do you need?" she heard Ernesto ask.

Pablo grinned. "Do you guys have any coffee?"

Ernesto groaned. "That's the only reason we agreed to this. We thought you had coffee."

"Sorry."

The pharmacy wasn't too big, and someone had managed to get the electricity up there. But there was only enough insulin in there for a couple of weeks. She stared at it crestfallen. All this work for a couple more weeks of life.

She emerged to find Ernesto still speaking to Pablo.

"Juana wants us to build more of these bridges. She wants to link all the villages around here. Eventually, she wants to reach Cusco. She says we've got plenty of cable."

"Cusco got bombed. Badly."

"I heard. Do you know who did it?"

Pablo shrugged. "The Chinese. The Americans. The Russians. The Brazilians. Who knows? All of them were fighting."

The war had fallen on them like a snowstorm out of a clear sky, spilling southward before the news of escalation even reached the far-flung Peruvian Andes. No one here knew what it was about, either.

"Have you got any drones?" Ernesto said.

"A couple. They don't fly."

"Karina and I'll take care of that. Every drone is worth its weight in gold. As long as we have drones, we can build our bridges in the sky. You said the nearest village is a hundred meters down?" He looked across the gap separating two peaks.

"Yeah, but they don't have a radio and only Carlos and Consuelo can get there without getting shot at. They're Argentine tourists who are expert rock climbers. All the actual roads are closed." He shuddered. "Those machines don't care about civilian casualties."

"I know. Can these Argentines take a message?"

"Of course."

"Wait. Better than that. Let's send them a radio."

Pablo looked at him quizzically. "Are you in a hurry?"

"I am." Karina blinked through the sudden tears. All that work for only another week's worth of insulin.

Ernesto hugged her. It wasn't the outcome they'd hoped for.

But now, again, they had to move quickly.

"Pablo, go get those Argentines." Ernesto said.

He rushed towards the cable car.

"Where are you going?"

"I'm going to grab the radio."

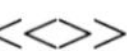

Juana made her only journey across the chasm three days later, everyone on both sides realizing that speed was of the essence.

The Argentines had carried the radio. The villagers on the other end had put up their anchor point that same day, and then the laborious process of transporting cable and winches across the first chasm began. There was only so much weight that anyone trusted to the basket and the original cable.

"Come with us," Ernesto said to Juana. "You're the heart of this project. You can twist everyone from here to Cusco to your bidding."

"I wish that was true but it's not. This is a job for young people. For you," she said. Then she turned to Karina and held out her hand. "There are old gods in these mountains. They brought you to us, and they kept you here against your will. You've done your part to help the people of the hills, and they'll do their part to see you safely back somewhere you can get your medicine. Don't lose faith."

Karina hugged Juana hard, silently. "Thank you," she said. "I can't believe all you're doing for me. You're the only reason I'm still alive."

Juana put her hand on Karina's mouth. "No. The reason you're alive is that you weren't on the road when the war came. You were lucky. We were all lucky." Then she looked around at the mountains surrounding them. "Or maybe I'm right and there is something watching over us."

"Maybe," Karina pressed Juana's hand.

The team from Concepción manhauled the cage onto the new cable. They'd spent the past two hours installing a brake—no one wanted to lose control on the downhill slope. It was bad enough that they would need to haul the cage up the wire every time they needed to ascend. Until they found a way to motorize this stretch, it would be a job for muscular folk only.

At least the trip down was easy.

Smiling, incredulous faces greeted them in the third village and helped them down from the cage.

"Do you have any insulin here?"

Confused heads shook.

"Then help us keep moving. Where's the nearest village to the south?"

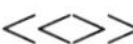

The syringes ran out four villages later, still thirty kilometers from Cusco.

Karina injected herself before lunch, and then slumped down to cry.

"Have some food," Ernesto said.

"Won't make much difference in the long run," she replied.

"You just took an injection. You have to eat."

They ate in silence until Karina lifted her head and said: "Could you leave me alone? I… I don't want to be with anyone right now."

But she soon found that she didn't want to be alone with her grief, but wanted, more than anything, to think about something else. Death was too close to dwell upon.

She headed into the village, where everyone was marveling at the new cable vehicle and making drawings of the cage so they could copy it when the one that Juana had ordered built in the first village up the line went inevitably ahead, blazing the highway in the mountains.

"How are you?" they asked.

Word of the sick girl who'd worked so hard to bring them together, to make the lives of the villagers better, had already spread among the thirty or forty people in the tiny hamlet. They'd opened their doors for her and offered every kind of comfort except the one she simply couldn't live without.

"Have you tried coca leaves in tea?" "Have you tried…" "Do you have…"

The babble of suggestions was met with sad shaking of the head. She knew they meant well, but none of them were truly knowledgeable about modern treatment.

She just shook her head. After a while, the desire to be alone returned, stronger than ever.

She found Ernesto sitting alone at the edge of the village. He looked up when she approached, the expression on his face mirroring her own; although he tried to put on a brave face when he saw her, he could do nothing about his red-rimmed eyes. She sat beside him and watched a cloud in the distance.

Despair pulled at her like a deep, black pit.

And suddenly, she laughed.

"What?" Ernesto said.

I just had a crazy idea. Just one of the industrial drones is enough to carry a hundred, hundred and fifty kilos, right? Or three or four of the medium-lifters?"

His eyes got big. "I'm almost afraid to ask why."

"I was thinking we could fly ourselves to Cusco."

"That's crazy."

"Maybe… but thirty kilometers is right at the edge of their range. Even the solar ones need battery life to lift any real weight. But what do I have to lose?"

"We. What do *we* have to lose," he said. "If you go, I'm going with you."

"You just said it was crazy."

"It is. But I said the same thing about the cable bridges."

She wanted to say no, to tell him to dedicate his life to helping the villagers, but she couldn't bring herself to say it. In the end, she just hugged him.

Then a thought struck her. "If we take the drones, they can't keep building the cable bridges."

"There are plenty of drones in the villages. It was how they brought up most of the materials. What they needed was the idea, and you supplied that."

"And how will they get them to receive radio signals?"

"Leave instructions for them. You're not the only programmer in Peru. I'm sure there's at least one in the villages. We've connected enough people that there has to be one, at least."

"But…"

He cut her off. "Do you want to die?"

She looked away.

"I didn't think so. Then let's do this. And I'm going with you, so if you even try to talk me out of it, I'll tie you up and drag you. You can have them send me to jail for kidnapping if we find a judge."

She hesitated for a long time. Ernesto didn't deserve to have to die for her. But finally, she nodded.

"Good. We have basically everything we need to build a harness. Cusco's bombed to pieces, but all we need is one standing pharmacy or working hospital."

She looked out into the distance, no longer thinking of her impending death but thinking of the journey ahead, calculating odds.

"It might be a rough flight. The wind through the mountains can be treacherous," she said.

Ernesto smiled at her. "Don't blame me. It was your idea."

They got to work.

<<>>

Karina, one arm badly scraped and barely able to hold herself upright, helped Ernesto as he limped into the tent on a possibly broken ankle. Inside the tent, a man in the green uniform of the Peruvian Army with a Red Cross band on his arm looked up from a desk. Cots surrounded him, but he was the only person in the large space. A generator hummed in the background. "You look like you need help," the man said.

Karina and Ernesto exchanged a look, as they sank down onto a cot.

"It was a rough landing," Ernesto said.

"Where did you fall from?"

"That's a long story, and you won't believe me. Is the army in control here?"

The man chuckled, a rueful sound. "If you call me, and one nurse and three soldiers the Army, then yes. As far as I know, we're the only surviving military unit in the whole of South America." A stern look followed. "Now get over here and let me treat your injuries."

"I don't have time," Karina said, not bothering to keep the desperation from her voice. "Do you have any insulin?"

"More than we could ever use, at least until it expires in a few months. Very few people survived the bombing of Cusco, and the diabetics didn't last long enough for us to get here. Only a handful survived. Sit. Let me test your blood sugar, and I'll get you a dose."

"Thank God," Ernesto said. This time, he didn't bother to hide his own tears.

Unable to control herself any further, Karina hugged him. "Thank you, thank you. I…" she didn't have the words and she broke down.

"Thank me?" Ernesto said. "How can you say that? You might have saved my entire people. What I did is nothing."

The doctor stared at them briefly, a look of disbelief on his features. "I want to hear this story after I get you dosed up," he said, doing a finger-stick to get a drop of blood.

"It's long."

"Does it look like I'm in a hurry? I would like nothing better than a good story."

Ernesto laughed. "I'll trade it for some real coffee."

"Real coffee? Do I look Colombian? The closest thing we have is long-expired instant from an army rations pack."

"We'll take it," he replied.

As the man opened a refrigerator to get the insulin, Ernesto turned to her. "What now?"

"We've got a highway to build." No stock of insulin would last forever, but she had time now.

That made her no better off than anyone else. But no worse, either.

Musings of a Tower Jockey

Bruce Golden

The whine of a straining engine,
The jolt of a familiar rut in the road,
Bodies sway and strain for balance
Each time the road curves
And the truck's tires slide.
Someone's steel pot
Batters aimlessly about.
There's a new face among us,
His expression taut with fear,
Eyes wide in disbelief
As the truck swerves
Around another corner.
He hasn't yet learned
To be unafraid of the knowledge
That the driver is stoned,
Or drunk,
Or just plain pissed.

A jarring stop.
I jump out.
A facsimile in green fatigues
Walks by without greeting.
I pass through barbed wire,
Pull the gate,
Snap the lock,
Glance up at steel girders,

Alternative War

Wooden planks,
And begin to climb.
On top I shed my ammo belt,
Drop my helmet and M16,
And squat on the sheet metal floor.

How many hours
Have I perched on that chilly surface,
Squinting at paperbacks
Smuggled under my shirt;
Or hunted for roaches among the dust
To roll a number;
Or read the bitter graffiti
Scrawled on walls
Battered by angry rifle butts and boots;
Or slept away the time
Knowing a rock thrown to the catwalk
Would be my alarm?

Better the fantasy of dreams
Or words
Or weed
Than time spent wondering
The reality or reason
Of my position,
Standing watch high above the world
In my tower,
Overlooking bunkers
Of bombs and missiles
In a foreign land,
And watching for the enemy.

Intruder

James Hancock

Glass cracked and slid from the back door. An old and frail frame, much like the man who lived there. Shards hit stone kitchen floor tiles; daggers shattering to slithers and splinters. The sound was sudden and obvious, cutting through the silence of night. There was no hiding it, but Mila had no intention of being unheard. She reached between glass teeth and into the mouth of the door, finding the lock. Click! She was in.

Wasting no time, she crunched over the broken fragments and headed into the house with purpose. Kitchen, hallway, and finally the living room. She switched on the light and took in her surroundings. A long room with Artex ceiling above Persian rugs, and bay windows at the far end. A wing armchair faced an old record player and handmade cabinet of stained oak, near to a sturdy bookcase lined with faded hardback tomes. An antique writing desk sat in perfect place at the nearest corner, with a faded leather chair pushed in close. The room was spacious, which gave it an unhomely feel. The open fireplace unused, the mantle serving as a glorified shelf for small ornaments. A normal family would easily house a three-piece suite and large television in the unused space. But this was no normal family. Far from it.

Mila stood in the centre of the room, taking in the aroma of leather, dusty books, and a hint of woody pipe smoke. The walls were bare. No paintings. No photos. No memories worth displaying.

She knew where to start; teasing fingertips across the line of trinkets and treasures which rested atop the fireplace, and stopping on a small china box. She lifted the lid. Inside was the prize. Nestled into a bed of crushed velvet was an old pocket watch. Dulled with age, and nothing particularly fancy to its craftsmanship. She took it out, gathered its chain with her other hand, and clicked it open.

She gazed at the engraved inscription inside.

With all my love, Helena. xx

A light came on and diverted Mila's attention to an old man hunched in the living room doorway. He appeared somewhat startled by the intruder who had broken in without a care for stealth or silence. Even though enveloped in a thick and cumbersome dressing gown, Mila could see the skeleton pushing tightly against his pale freckled skin, and sunken eyes below a head of thinned white hair. Wealth had bought the best care, and seen him well into his nineties, but the man looked like a ghost.

The room remained silent as eyes fixed upon eyes before the old man glanced down at the watch in Mila's hand, and to the pistol she slid free from under her coat. She was no common burglar, she had purpose, and the gun was essential to her task. Mila wouldn't shoot a man, especially an old man, without good reason. She had good reason.

"Who are you? What do you want?" the old man's accent held a trace of German, with the sharpness hidden, or ironed out over decades of living away from the Motherland. His expression was sour and his glare cut deep.

Two simple questions. Mila knew he didn't want the answers.

"Can you hear me?" the old man snapped. "Right, I am calling the police!" He began crossing the room towards a phone in the corner, but stopped as Mila raised her pistol to aim at him.

"Wilhelm Gruber?" Mila asked in a light and pleasant tone. She afforded herself a calm and collected smile. She already knew the answer. She wouldn't be here if there was any uncertainty of the man she had before her.

The old man glared at Mila. "My name is William Graber. You've got the wrong house. You've got the wrong man!"

Mila's smile dropped, and she shook her head. "No. Lieutenant Wilhelm Gruber. Stationed in Belgium until nineteen forty-two, and then Poland for the remainder of the war..."

"Nonsense!" the old man interrupted. "You don't know what you're talking about."

Mila's eyes were dark. She spoke through gritted teeth of rage, her voice rising in volume with each word... "Murderer! Thief! Coward! Nazi!"

The final word hung in the room as they stared at each other. Mila, with tears welling in her eyes as the conclusion of her long search neared its fruition. And Gruber, who was clearly aware there was no talking his way out of this.

"Dogs; that's what they were to you. Not even human. Millions of brilliant lives stolen and the surviving families ruined. What gave you the right?" Tears rolled down Mila's cheeks as she read the words inside the watch again. "I'd say you will join them soon, but that would be a lie. You'll be going somewhere else. Into the dark..."

Gruber interrupted with an exaggerated yawn. "You talk too much. Your people always did".

Mila shut the watch case and returned her attention to the creature before her. Any doubt in her actions removed by Gruber's venomous tongue.

He nodded and gave a cocky smile. "You know, this isn't the first time I've had a gun pointed at me."

Mila stared at him. No need to speak. Let him have his final say.

"You think I fear death, young lady? At my age, it is just a waiting game." He huffed disappointment and looked at her with disgust.

Mila held up the pocket watch. The last thing Gruber would see. "I've come for my grandfather's watch, Obersturmbannführer Gruber." She aimed her pistol at his head. "Your wait is over".

Without hesitation, she squeezed the trigger.

AWOL

Philip Brian Hall

Jackie Carnegie stepped down from her battered all-terrain vehicle and stood in the dusty road, watching her death climb into the morning sky. From the spaceport on the far side of Murdoch, a long, thin needle rose steadily atop a livid column of flame. The last troopship was leaving Kyron.

They hadn't waited. Why should they? She'd gone absent without leave; they didn't know where, and they couldn't spare the time to search. Nobody's fault but her own, right from the beginning. She could hardly blame the MPs who'd caught her smuggling in contraband with the President's personal supplies. And nobody had forced her to leave the base and get stinking drunk as soon as she got out of the stockade, or to sleep it off at her girlfriend's place rather than back in the barracks.

"Jackie, is it true?" Rosita had said to her the next morning. "Maria just called to tell me your Marines are returning to base. She says a troop carrier landed at first light."

Jackie groaned and turned over sleepily amid the tangled sheets. "How would I know?" she grumbled. Her head hurt.

"Surely you're in touch with someone? You always hear what's going on. Could they be pulling out?"

"Not a chance. We've been allied with Kyron forever."

"But Maria says the Seabees have gone aboard. There's only a skeleton force guarding the perimeter."

"She says what?" Abruptly awake, Jackie rolled out of bed, dragged on her uniform, sprinted for the ATV parked outside... and arrived one hour late.

<<>>

Abandoned vehicles choked the motor pool, booby-trapped just like the ammunition dumps. Jackie knew the safe ways around both. Within fifteen minutes, she'd equipped herself with a portable arsenal, stuffed a backpack with rations and survival gear, and parked the ATV among twenty others of its kind. She regretted parting with her transport, but if Hunsa scouts spotted it elsewhere, they'd draw the obvious conclusion.

Jackie set out on foot across country towards the Nandi Hills, from Murdoch little more than a shimmering, blue luminescence on the horizon beyond the great plain. It was just after noon. Kyron's twin suns raised the temperature beyond blood heat, but it was dry. Sparse, spiky vegetation straggling over red soil scarcely impeded her progress. The going was yielding and conditions tolerable by Marine standards. By mid-afternoon, she'd put ten klicks between herself and the spaceport, safe enough to rest in the shade of an oasis while she assessed her situation.

The broad, leathery leaves of the thirty-foot trees concealed ripe fruit. She could hunt, fish and trap; once she made it to the hills, living off the land would be easy.

No one would expect her to do anything but lay low. What would've happened if she'd made it back in time? She'd have been thrown in the brig, that's what.

Jackie possessed the skills to make herself a nuisance to the invaders from space if she chose. She'd completed special forces training before figuring out the relative merits of military and private enterprise. She *could* damage them. Before they caught her.

The truth was, with no support and no way of getting off Kyron, she couldn't survive in the long run, whichever choice she made. She'd known that from the moment she'd watched the troopship disappear. Time was on the enemy's side.

The rumble of multiple engines disturbed Jackie's contemplation of her life's lopsided balance sheet. A mile east, a column of Hunsa tanks and armored personnel carriers was advancing openly on Murdoch by the main road.

Jackie ground her teeth. The invaders should pay for this. If only she had a helicopter gunship. But she didn't. Although alone she might kill half a dozen before artillery fire landed on her position, she'd have no chance of subsequent escape across open country.

No. If she decided to fight, she needed to await a better opportunity. As the dust settled behind the convoy, she shouldered her pack and set off again towards the hills.

<<>>

A watcher, close to the highest summit of the Nandi range, naively betrayed his position by allowing sunlight to glitter from his lens. The Marine shook her head. It was evidently a day for military ineptitude.

She continued in a straight line until she found a transverse gully offering dead ground from the observer's elevation, then she circled to the left and climbed the scree-strewn rear slope.

The absence of lookouts told Jackie the interlopers were few. She already knew they lacked military smarts. All the same, as she peered carefully out from behind a jumble of boulders on the ridge, she was surprised to find the watcher still in place.

A young, brunette Kyronese, wearing a city-dweller's idea of country clothing: jeans, cowboy boots, and a check shirt, lay propped on her elbows, binoculars to her eyes, rucksack by her side. She was alone. And the best-known female celebrity on the planet.

"Why, Miss Valerian, fancy meeting you here," Jackie said, stepping out.

The girl turned over, tried to get up, lost her balance, and ended up sitting gracelessly on her behind. "What... who? My God, Jackie Carnegie! Who let you out of jail?" She got to her feet, dusting off her pants with every show of annoyance, but Jackie suspected she saw relief in the dark brown eyes.

"I got out for bad behavior," Jackie lied brazenly, lowering her sniper rifle. She wasn't about to admit the truth, was she? "The jailers' behavior, that is. They went home and left me."

"My parents and the rest of the government went with them," the girl snorted angrily.

"But you didn't?"

"Oh, you noticed? Somebody has to stay and fight."

Jackie smiled ruefully. “Pardon me, Miss Valerian, I saw you as a society girl, not a resistance leader.”

“Don't be a jackass!” Her eyes flashed. “I’m not stupid. I know someone with no military experience can’t become a guerrilla overnight. I’m going to need help. And stop calling me *Miss Valerian*. It makes me sound like a damned high school teacher.”

“Should I call you Katy?”

“Everyone else does. Look, I'm a famous face; you know that. And for some reason, I'm popular. If I can rally some fighters around me, I'll be a figurehead with whom people can identify.”

“Dressed like that, you're more likely to be a target the Hunsa identify,” Jackie remarked laconically, “from about a mile away. Did you bring any less conspicuous clothes?”

<<>>

Katy's transport was just inside the tree line, where she'd turned off a rutted side-road leading down to the little town of Blake's Bridge. The vehicle was well-concealed from aerial surveillance but not exactly ideal for getting about without attracting attention.

“I see you borrowed your father's car,” Jackie said.

“I was in a hurry, and there wasn't a lot of choice,” Katy snapped. “Why, what's wrong with it?”

“A stretch, off-road SUV with a big sliding roof so the president can stand up and wave to the crowds? Why nothing at all. Who could possibly notice a vehicle like that out here in the sticks?”

“That was sort of the idea,” Katy protested. “How am I going to collect followers unless people know where I am?”

“I see. You maybe expect the Hunsa to do nothing while you gather this support? You might as well stand on a soapbox in Murdoch's main square with a sign around your neck saying, *'Here I am—Shoot me!'*"

“All right guerrilla mastermind! If you know so much, suppose you tell me how we start a resistance?”

“Hey, hold it a minute. Where did that 'we' come from? I'm not Kyronese. I got no stake in this.”

“Typical!” Katy's tone oozed contempt. “I should've known better. I expect you only took the job guarding my father to get away from the front. Then you find your way into the safety of the stockade as soon as the Hunsa get within a hundred miles."

"Yeah, well, my bootlegging business didn't work out so good," Jackie conceded, her face reddening. Realizing her tale of abandonment by the guards sounded flimsy, she improvised a little more. "And I was underground, trying to tunnel my way out of the stockade, when everyone left. Otherwise, I would've been evacuated this morning."

"So you're stuck here. What are you aiming to do? Watch my people die?"

"The way I see it, Axel Heimer and his boys never hurt me personally."

"Oh, so you just figure on laying low? Waiting for what, Jackie? There's no help coming. It'll maybe take a while, but when there are no Kyronese left to help you and the Hunsa come calling, will you still believe you made the right choice?"

Jackie remained silent. She'd nothing to say; Katy's logic was sound.

"You could be a big help to us, Jackie."

"To *us*, you say?"

"Okay, to *me*. You may be a crook, but you're a Marine. You know a heap more than I do. As you've so thoughtfully pointed out, I don't even know where to start."

Jackie drew patterns in the dust with the toe of her boot. Sucking in air through her teeth, she raised her head.

"Make no mistake, Jackie," Katy said, "with you or without you, I'm going to do what I can. I may go down, almost certainly will, but I'm going down fighting!"

Jackie looked down at the dust again. The silence stretched out uncomfortably.

"Dammit, you bitch, say something!" Katy exclaimed.

"Okay. What do you say we bury the hatchet? Neither of us can do anything tonight. Tomorrow will be soon enough to figure out where we go from here."

Katy gave her an appraising look. "I can live with that," she said.

<<>>

"I don't get it," Katy said. "The town's clear. What's to stop us walking right in there?"

The two of them were up on a scrub-covered hilltop outside Blake's Bridge. Katy was looking at the town through her binoculars and Jackie through her spotter scope.

"One thousand yards to the main street outside the mayor's office," Jackie muttered. "Drop seventy-five feet. Wind 5 mph from the left."

"Jackie!" Katy exclaimed. "You're not listening to me."

"I'm sorry, Katy, did you say something?"

"Dammit, Jackie! I asked why we don't just head into town. What are you doing anyway?"

"In answer to both questions, the Hunsa have established themselves in Murdoch. They're sending out small teams to take charge of the main settlements. They don't expect trouble in Blake's Bridge."

"How do you know this?"

"First, because the Hunsa are stupid; they're using open radio, not even coding their messages. My Hunsa ain't so good, but I got enough."

"And second?"

"Be careful not to point your binoculars into the lower sun. You'll see a single ATV with two soldiers in it heading towards town. A couple of miles down the Murdoch Road."

Katy swung her binoculars. "I see them. And how does this explain what you were doing?"

"Well, assuming you don't want to do a whole heap of walking, we need less conspicuous transport. That ATV and those uniforms would make us nearly invisible to the Hunsa. But since they aren't going to hand them over, we'll have to take them."

"You think you can kill two Hunsa from a thousand yards?"

"DOPE says yes."

"Anybody *but* a dope would try and get closer."

"No, No. Not *a* dope, DOPE, *Data On Previous Engagements*. It's software that does the math and tells me where to aim, allowing for elevation, trajectory decay, windage, and so on."

"Don't tell me you're a sniper!"

"Okay, I won't. A thousand yards is child's play for a real sniper. But I'm good enough."

“Jackie, look at me.” Katy’s tone was suddenly earnest.

Jackie rolled onto her side. “Yes, ma'am.”

“This is a long road. No chance of turning back. Are you sure?”

“Hell,” Jackie said. “Who wants to live forever? More to the point, Miss Valerian...”

“Katy.”

“More to the point, Katy, are *you* sure? We won’t just be committing ourselves; we’re committing the innocent folk of Blake’s Bridge. Without asking them. I don’t have the right.”

“That’s my responsibility, Jackie. No one else can carry it for me. And I’m sure.”

“Very well. Then you look after the politics, Katy. I’ll fight your war for you.”

Katy smiled grimly. “Welcome to the Kyronese resistance, sergeant. Glad to have you.” There was no doubt in her eyes. She looked at Jackie differently from the night before.

<<>>

When Jackie and Katy walked into Blake's Bridge, the body of the Hunsa officer was lying in the dirt of the main street. Her driver still sat behind the wheel as though asleep.

A crowd had gathered in a circle in front of the clapboard buildings. No one had taken any initiative.

“Who could've done it?” The speaker was a grizzled, middle-aged man in mechanic's coveralls. “It said on the news our army surrendered.”

“I heard the Hunsa turned Valerian Stadium into a Prisoner-of-War camp,” added a woman wearing a shopkeeper's apron. “And the Earth Marines just cut and ran—left us to their tender mercies.”

“Not entirely.” Jackie pushed her way through, sniper rifle slung over her shoulder, and knelt beside the officer to check she was dead. “Non-essential personnel were evacuated, sure. Specialists like me stayed behind to help you organize resistance.”

“Did you make those two shots, girl?” The mechanic smiled his approval at Jackie. “Bravo! Fancy shooting.”

“Sure,” the shopkeeper interrupted. “Fancy enough to bring reprisals down on the whole town. You heard Heimer’s threats.”

"If the regular army can't beat the Hunsa, what chance do we have?" another woman called out.

"Who said there's gonna be a resistance, anyway?" the mechanic asked.

"That would be me," said Katy, following Jackie into the center of the circle, accompanied by a chorus of gasps and whispers of her name.

"Okay, you're worried about reprisals," Katy said. "I agree it's what you'd expect from Heimer; it's been the pattern on other planets the Hunsa conquered. But these two stiffs didn't get time to make any calls. As far as you're concerned, they never arrived. Since you didn't know they were on their way, naturally you won't report their non-arrival. Sergeant Carnegie and I will take away the ATV and the bodies. The only way the Hunsa learn what happened is if one of you tells them."

"No-one here's gonna do that, Katy," the mechanic affirmed.

"I'm afraid that might depend on how nicely you're asked," Jackie butted in. She dragged the driver out of his seat and hauled the body round to the back of the vehicle, the heels of his jackboots scraping parallel tracks in the murram road. "Heimer's Secret Police can be persuasive, I'm told. Safer if you assume the worst. The Hunsa *will* find out what happened *and* that Katy was here. So if you stay here, you might get shot."

A murmur ran around the crowd.

"Now, if you want to follow us up into the Nandi Hills and join the resistance," Jackie continued, "most likely you'll still get shot. But with luck, you'll take some of the bastards with you."

"My father's too old to live rough, or he'd be here with us," Katy said. "You'll have to make do with me. I can't promise you anything except this: I'll liberate Kyron or die trying. If any of you feel the same, come up into the hills and find us. We'll be waiting."

Jackie dumped the second body in the back of the ATV; Katy climbed into the driver's seat and gunned the engine. As soon as Jackie got in, the car shot off up the road in a cloud of red dust.

“Nice speech,” Jackie said.

“I damn well meant it. I'll do whatever's necessary. Anything. You better believe it.”

“Oh, I do,” Jackie smiled. “So help me, I do!”

<<>>

When the first of Kyron's suns set in the evening, the second remained in the sky for about twenty minutes. The locals called the resulting half-light *ghostfall.* Daytime businesses closed, and daytime people headed home before dark.

Three days' observation persuaded Jackie the Hunsa had foolishly chosen the second sunset instead of the first to schedule guard change on the abandoned Earth motor pool. In addition, two or three scrap-strewn craters in the black tarmac marked the site of attempts to disarm booby traps. The place smelled of burnt metal and blood. Rather than lose any more bomb-disposal technicians, the Hunsa sealed up the pool and guarded the gates.

During ghostfall on the fourth day, Jerome, the mechanic, and another recently-recruited rebel drove Jackie and Katy into Murdoch in the captured ATV. Jerome and his companion wore the Hunsa uniforms. Jackie reckoned in the weak light the tired guards, ready and waiting for their relief, would take the insurgents for their own people.

Jackie wore her Marine uniform and a lot of dark makeup, suggesting she'd suffered a beating. She lolled in her seat as though barely conscious.

Katy wore civilian dress. She carried a stolen secret police ID and forged orders in the style of those found on the dead officer.

For Jackie, Katy shouldn't have been there at all. As the figurehead of their nascent resistance, she was far too valuable. Yet they had to equip their growing band of fighters somehow, and no one else spoke Hunsa.

When the ATV pulled up at the motor pool gates, the uniformed passenger got out. Ignoring the gate guards, he scurried round to Katy's door and held it open. In fluent Hunsa, she berated him.

"Idiot! Why don't you tell the man what we're here for? Do I have to do everything myself? Oh, for pity's sake, get out of the way."

Katy got out of the ATV and marched angrily up to the gate.

"You there—which of you's in charge here?"

A worried-looking corporal stepped forward.

"You've been told to expect us?" Katy said.

The corporal looked more worried. He shook his head.

"Good God, I'm surrounded by imbeciles! Can no one in this army do anything right?" Katy waved her ID under his nose. "Look, I'm Bronstein, Internal Security. I have a prisoner who knows how to disarm the bombs attached to these vehicles. Only she was a trifle hard to persuade. I don't think she'll last the night. I've brought her here so she can show us before she dies. Do you understand?"

"Certainly, ma'am."

"Thank goodness! Someone with a few brain cells." She took out her forged orders. "Right. Here's my authorization. I need you to unlock the gates for us. When the prisoner's disarmed the first bomb, we're going to take away the vehicle so our techs can examine it properly back at base. Have you got that?"

"Yes, ma'am."

"Good man. I'll put in a word for you. What's your name?"

"Weisser, ma'am. Corporal Henreid Weisser, 5th Armored Cavalry."

Katy scribbled illegibly on the paper. "Good. I've made a note of that. Now let us in before we lose the light." She started back to the ATV. "Oh, and Henreid," she half-turned back, "do be sure and tell your relief about us. I don't need any half-wits shooting at us when we come out."

<<>>

Jackie looked over the truck driver's shoulder as they slowed. "What's wrong?" she said.

"Roadblock," Jerome replied. "Probably just a spot check."

"How many guards?"

"Two dozen, maybe three?"

"Spot check my foot! Get ready to floor it." Jackie had positioned a tripod-mounted heavy machine gun pointing out the back of the truck in anticipation of pursuit. She cast off its transport lashings, then came back and peered over Jerome's shoulder. The ATV in front of them had come to a halt. Katy appeared to be reprising her secret police routine.

"No, no," Jackie breathed. "Don't get out of the car... oh, shit!"

Katy was stomping around, shouting and gesticulating, waving her orders. The girl had guts to burn, but the guards weren't buying the act. Three of them ordered the driver out of the ATV at gunpoint.

"See the gap where the two APCs are reversed together across the road?" Jackie said to Jerome.

"Yes. It looks all of three feet wide."

"The center of gravity of those things is just behind the engine. If you hit the middle of that gap at thirty miles an hour, you'll push both of them out of the way and bust right through."

"What about Katy and Paco?"

"No chance. Too many guards and they're already alert. We can maybe save the weapons; if we try to save Katy and Paco as well, we'll all be dead one minute from now."

"But..."

"No buts. Wait for my word. When I say *Go!* Give me all you've got, and don't stop for anything."

A Hunsa officer instructed his troops to secure the two prisoners and take them to his command car, parked well off the road. Paco looked scared. Katy struggled and raged, still trying to carry off her hopeless deception. Five soldiers started down the road towards the truck, guns at the ready. Jackie let them get just over halfway.

"Go!" she said.

Engine roaring, the truck leaped forward. Two soldiers flung themselves out of the way; three stood their ground and started shooting. Badly-aimed bullets starred the windscreen. Impacts, shouts, bucking over bodies. Shots from the side. A horrendous smash as the hood plowed into the barricade, shouldering aside both the smaller vehicles as

Jackie had predicted. Screams of rending metal mingled with the cries of wounded and dying men.

Then they were through and still accelerating, raising a dust cloud, leaving the surviving guards in chaos as Jackie's heavy machine gun sprayed death in their wake.

<<>>

"They're alive," said Viola, the shopkeeper. "No thanks to you."

Viola was florid of complexion and overweight. The trek up into the Nandi Hills from Blake's Bridge had left her perspiring and breathing heavily. She sat down on a hummock of grass, mopped her brow with her apron, and glared at Jackie.

"There's no call for that attitude, Viola," said Jerome, the mechanic. "I was there too, you know. What d'you suppose the two of us could have done against twenty or thirty Hunsa? We were lucky to get away with our lives."

"All I'm saying is, Katy should never have been there!" insisted Viola.

"But she's alive," Jackie interjected. "Do you know where they're being held?"

"Katy's in The Red House. The secret police have turned the East Wing into a prison. The Hunsa have taken over the West Wing for their general staff; they reckon Axel Heimer himself is expected in the next few days."

"Uh-huh. What about Paco?"

"Paco's locked up in the old police station."

"You know this for sure?"

"Why do you suppose I'm here? Bernardo came in from Murdoch with the garbage truck this morning. He'd been collecting around The Red House earlier. He says the Hunsa know who Katy is. They've given her twenty-four hours to broadcast a call for all guerrillas to surrender, or they'll execute Paco."

"So we have to get her out tonight," said Jerome.

"No," Jackie smiled grimly. That's what they'll be expecting; we'd walk straight into a trap. First things first: we take away their leverage. We spring Paco."

<<>>

The armed guard outside the police station saluted smartly and held open the door. Stiffly, Jackie marched in. She wore a long black leather trench coat over a Hunsa captain's uniform. With her hair scraped severely back into a tight bun, she hoped she looked sufficiently like one of the aristocrats who populated the Hunsa general staff.

The old police reception desk was unstaffed. Behind the glass screen, three soldiers in shirtsleeves sat around a table playing a card game. There were beer cans open on the table. The door that gave admission to the holding cells was behind them.

Jackie took off her leather gloves and slapped them noisily from one hand to the other. Startled by the unexpected sight, the three guards sprang to their feet and stood to attention.

Jackie glared at them furiously, scowling, apparently too angry to speak.

One of the guards began to talk in an apologetic tone. Jackie had no idea what the man was saying. She silenced him with a grunt, pointing angrily to the security door that separated the vestibule from the staff area. The guard hastened to open it. Jackie stalked through and paced slowly up to the card table. She stared at the cards, at the beer, around the room. The guards quailed.

Fortunately for Jackie, whose acting talents were stretched, the brief distraction allowed four other rebels to subdue the sentry and enter the police station. The astonished guards never had a chance to resist. While the newcomers kept them covered and began to tie them up, Jackie unlocked the door to the cells.

Paco was bruised and bleeding; his legs wobbled when he stood; his mumbled words made no sense. Two rebels helped him out through the door of the police station and into the waiting vehicle. Jackie looked all around to check they'd left nothing that might give the Hunsa a clue to their identity. As she was closing the door behind her, a buzzer sounded on the switchboard.

“That's torn it!” said Jerome.

“Not necessarily. When the top brass get no reply, they'll send reinforcements down here from The Red House. Maybe that'll leave them short-handed enough for me to sneak in. I'll just recce the place and where they're holding Katy. I'll see you back in Nandi."

<<>>

The guard bringing Katy her evening meal got a mouthful of abuse for her pains. The prisoner lay on a cot in her cell, not even turning to look at the food.

"It probably is shit at that," Jackie replied, "but it's no use cursing me in Hunsa; I don't know what you're saying."

"Jackie?" Katy rolled over in an instant and flung herself towards the bars. "What the Hell are you doing here? How'd you get in?"

"Oh, I've been sneaking past MPs for a very long time, Katy. 'Course they were usually on the same side as me, in a manner of speaking."

"Can you get me out?"

"Hell, no! I bluffed my way in without speaking, but there's no way I can bluff my way out with you. What I can do is get you into the West Wing. You know that place better than most. Tell me where we can hide."

<<>>

"I don't know." Katy shrugged apologetically. "I thought this space was a lot bigger the last time." Wriggling her hips, she was just able to get high enough inside the replica monster's hollow head to look out through its smoked glass eyes. The Kyron Presidential Museum's prehistoric reptile gallery remained deserted. The Hunsa weren't keen on paleontology.

"How old were you at the time?" Jackie coughed as a shower of dust landed on her face. She'd squeezed uncomfortably into the huge sauroid's gloomy chest cavity.

"About eight, I think."

"Yeah, right. Well, it'll do for now. When the Hunsa find you've escaped, they'll not waste a lot of time searching inside the building."

"Not for me, no, but their security will be all over the place in preparation for Heimer's visit."

"Damn! Is he really coming? Viola said so. I thought it was far too soon, straight after a rebel raid on Murdoch and all."

"He's coming to meet *me*. He has notions of me heading a puppet Kyronese government with him pulling my strings."

"You don't care to be a marionette?"

"I spat in my interrogator's eye. That's why I was in the cells rather than under house arrest in my suite."

Jackie chuckled. "As Danton said, *Audacity, always audacity*!"

"Who's Danton?"

"French revolutionary- a thousand years ago. Still good tactics. What would the enemy least expect? If we can stay hidden until Heimer and his henchmen turn up, we'll have a chance of doing something spectacular."

"You're mad!"

Jackie nodded. "Oh yes," she said. "So was Danton."

<<>>

While Axel Heimer's motorcade drove between the spaceport and The Red House, the troops guarding the latter assembled on parade. The perimeter guards were on the lookout for terrorists. They paid no attention when another squad of troopers turned up for the inspection. Jackie let out the breath she'd been holding as she watched Jerome and five of his fellow rebels quick march in goose-step, arms shouldered, to a side door of The West Wing.

With Katy handcuffed between two rebels and Jackie in her captain's uniform taking the lead, the eight insurgents marched out onto the parade ground just as the dictator's limousine came through the gates. Jackie reckoned no one would question a squad delivering the celebrity prisoner to Heimer, even if it wasn't exactly on the schedule for the day. Everyone would suppose someone else had ordered it.

"Remember—audacity," Jackie hissed. "We're all doing what we're supposed to do. Don't look so worried!"

Since no one can understand what an officer shouts on parade, she risked a few words of Hunsa, bawled at the top of her voice, as the little group approached the point where the car was about to draw up.

"Squ-a-a-a-d... Halt! Squ-a-a-a-d... Att-e-e-en... shun!"

The rebels managed an acceptable halt and presented arms as a confused driver held open the car door for Heimer. The pompous autocrat stepped out, wearing a sky-blue uniform and an array of medals that would have taken a real veteran thirty years to accumulate. His piggy eyes glittered with delight.

"Good! Excellent, captain!"

From the tone of the little man's voice, Jackie deduced she'd been commended. She snapped off a crisp salute.

"And you, I assume, are Miss Valerian?" Heimer walked up to Katy with a smile. "But my dear, you should not be in handcuffs." He turned to Jerome on her left. "Release her at once!"

Before Jerome's hesitation could arouse suspicion, Katy shook the cuffs at him. He hastened to free both her hands.

"And now, my dear, you must come and have lunch with me. We can get better acquainted. Please wait a few moments while I inspect the guard of honor."

"You son-of-a-bitch, I have a bomb strapped around my waist." Katy gave the dictator her most charming smile. "If you move more than ten feet away, I'll detonate it. What's left of your guard of honor won't find enough pieces of you to bury." Hidden from the greeting party by Heimer and Jackie, she undid a lower button of her blouse, exposing a suicide belt.

The color drained from Heimer's face, but he retained enough sense not to run or call for assistance. "What do you want?"

"You're going to invite me to show you around the city. We'll just walk out the gates arm in arm, chatting like the good friends we are. Leave your guards and instruct my jailers here to follow us at a discreet distance. No one else is to follow. Have you got that?"

Heimer nodded, his face frozen.

"No, no. This is such an amusing proposal that you will smile..." Katy continued. "I said smile, you bastard, or so help me I'll blow us all to Hell right here and now."

<<>>

Jackie Carnegie stepped down from the presidential stretch SUV and stood in the dusty road watching her unexpected reprieve climb into the sky. From the spaceport, a long, thin needle rose steadily atop a column of livid flame. The last Hunsa troopship was leaving Kyron.

"I suppose we have to let Heimer go now?" Katy said as she got down and stood beside her.

"He'll not dare invade again while he's reliant on us for monthly injections of the antidote," Jackie said. "By the time his doctors prove he never *was* infected with some undetectable Kyronese disease, the Earth forces will be back here. Between them and us, we'll soon have this planet impregnable."

"Jackie?"

"What?"

"You just called the Earth forces *them* and the Kyronese *us*."

"Did I? Well, maybe that's because I'm relying on you to keep me out of the brig. I'm still officially AWOL, you know."

"I'd like to think you had better reasons than that, Jackie."

"Oh? Well, it's true, I've grown fond of Kyron. When you're willing to die for a place, you do get that way, I suppose. And I've made friends here, of course. One in particular."

Katy gave her an appraising look. "I can live with that," she said.

Burden of Command

Karl El-Koura

When C Company didn't arrive as scheduled, Lieutenant Keph Tellart, commander of B Company, knew he was in trouble.

He and his team had been a year in the Hold. The mission was simple: defend the portal that separated this earth from Real Earth. The portal lay at the center of the compound, floating just above the brackish water. A door into Real Earth available to whatever threat this world held.

His team was ready to go home and leave this swamp, with its collection of pre-fabs, unbreathable air, and toothy critters. So was he, but without relief, he dared not leave. This crappy little pile of floating buildings was the first line of defense for Real Earth. Defense from what? That was hard to say, the auto guns on the perimeter, officially designated as sentinels, made short work of the local wildlife.

Generally.

Leapers were the only real difficulty, a creature like a giant spider with two dog-like heads, that could stride along the surface of the water through the stalks of grass with frightful speed and, as previous expeditions had learned, could take out an armor-clad soldier. No one wanted them on Real Earth; that was why they were in the Hold in the first place.

He had a good crew, the two sergeants and their teams focused on their work. Defending the portal. About fifty feet outside their floating island of cubes, the sentinels, a dozen automatic turrets, ever-vigilant to anything that dared approach from swamp or sky (there was no land in shooting distance). Maintaining these was a key activity. The needle-cone ammo needed replacement. Sensors needed cleaning. The work got done.

Relief was a week overdue when Sergeant Jasek entered his office and closed the door. He groaned. He knew she considered herself the official spokesman for the enlisted.

“Sir,” she said, “we need to send a distress signal.”

“We're not in distress,” Keph said. “We have adequate supplies. This is an anticipated scenario.” Enough supplies to last us three months, he thought. And then what? “Standing orders say that relief can be up to thirty days late, dependent on portal conditions, and we don’t know what the conditions are on the other side. There might be a tornado surrounding the portal—or something.”

“Or something,” she said. “I’d like to begin contingency planning.”

He turned his chair and grabbed a binder off the shelf. “Be my guest.” He thrust the binder towards her.

At thirty days she was back, a draft communication in her hand.

He gave it a cursory read. “Send it, Sergeant.” He gestured towards his console. “I’ll approve it when it comes through and let you know when—if—we get a response.”

Thirteen days later there was no response.

At shift change, the evening of that forty-third day, Jasek asked if she could speak privately with him. The look on her face as she closed the door to his office told him he couldn't delay a decision any longer.

“Lieutenant,” she said. “Protocol is to send a scout mission through the portal.”

He didn't respond immediately; he knew the protocol, but he had the discretion of command. It was clear that what was supposed to happen—three boats to emerge *from* the portal, full of food and other essential supplies that would keep the water pure and the sentinels working, with a squad of soldiers ready to relieve them—hadn’t happened.

She launched into a clearly rehearsed argument about their dwindling supplies and the need to check up on Real Earth.

“One person could...”

Keph held up his hand. “I agree with you about the need. But no one goes out alone. Are you thinking you'd go?”

“No, Sir,” Jasek said. “I promised Sergeant Prat I wouldn't if I managed to convince you. And my unit already said they'd stay here with me.”

“Fine,” Keph said. “I'll talk to Sergeant Prat.”

Prat and his team left the following night, after Keph had given them a long and probably unnecessary pep-talk.

He, Jasek and the privates watched on the screen in Ops. The boat silently cut through the stalks of tall grass toward the nearly invisible portal, then disappeared bow-first into it.

He'd sent them out as a team because it was protocol, yes. And, secondly, three people had a better chance of defending themselves, and maybe getting word back.

The precautions hadn’t mattered. Another week passed, and nothing. Jasek, binder pointedly in hand, followed him into his office again.

“So,” he said. “You have contingencies worked out?”

She briefed him like he was a cadet. He let her.

“I see three options,” she began. “One, keep waiting; two, abandon the station; three, close the portal by destroying the station, blowing up Operations.” He wanted to see them each on their own.

She did not disappoint and explained them in detail.

Her third option bothered him the most. Ops was sometimes called the Bomb Room because of the powerful explosives that lined its ceiling. But those bombs were a suicidal worst-case-scenario contingency, to be activated only if the Hold were overwhelmed. The idea was that the force of the explosion would close the portal, sealing it up like a flame will fuse two pieces of rope together. Unfortunately, it had no remote option—accessible to them, anyway.

He shook his head. “Options two and three are complete non-starters: for option two, without B Company—what’s left of it, anyway—repairing and replenishing the sentinels, Real Earth and its people will be harassed by leapers and any other creatures from this earth we haven’t seen yet in addition to whatever issues they're currently facing. Option three means blowing ourselves up, and I don’t think we’re at that point yet.”

Jasek acknowledged the issues. He was pleased with that. He could already feel the strain on the chain of command in her face. Nothing about the job was easy, and now she was seeing that as well.

"Let me work with the unit," she said. "We'll come up with something else."

Three days later, she presented him with a fourth option: close the portal from the other side.

"That's not possible," he said. According to the manual, the self-destruct sequence was complicated and required biometric—so on-site—activation. He had no doubt that Command could activate the self-destruct remotely; would they have risked sending a few soldiers and a dozen sentinels without a back-up plan if the Hold's company died and creatures began pouring out of a portal? But even knowledge of the existence of such a mechanism was levels above his pay grade.

"Private Chi thinks he's found a way."

"And if he's wrong?"

"We come back and blow ourselves up. Or fight until we run out of ammo and become leaper food. The options are endless." She smiled. An actual smile, if somewhat ironic.

"We can't risk it," Keph said. "And besides, I don't have authorization to close the portal." The smile disappeared.

"Why? Because someone we'll never meet has decided they'll be able to exploit this planet at some point, for their own benefit and certainly not ours?" She leaned back in the chair, and he knew her growing unease with his leadership had reached a breaking point. "We're running out of food and water. We have bullets to last another three weeks maybe? The attacks have become more frequent, so probably less than that. It's time to get out of here, Keph."

"Lieutenant," he corrected, though he'd never done that before. She straightened in her chair. "Our job is to defend this portal, make sure none of those things get through. We stay at our post until we're relieved, like we were taught to do. Listen"—he allowed his voice to soften—"we give Command another week, maybe two, to reply to our messages. If the situation hasn't changed by then, they can't fault us for crossing over. In the meantime, we stay and repair those sentinels when they need it and fill them up with bullets when they run out."

"Yes, Lieutenant." She seemed unconvinced and that night, in bed, Keph wondered if they'd sneak away in one of the boats, and he'd find himself alone in the Hold in the morning. Did he even remember how to put on a bodysuit? Although Swamp Earth had characteristics very similar to their own planet (it was the same planet, after all) the swamp in this part of the world puffed up enough toxic gases that breathing unfiltered air was strongly discouraged. Nobody had died, but he didn't want to have parasites scraped out of his lungs. Did he remember how to fix a sentinel? Without supplies, did it even matter?

The next day, he was relieved to see the three soldiers hunched over the table in the Mess, eating breakfast. He was still in command. For now.

Eight days later, he summoned Sergeant Jasek and Private Chi to his office.

"So what's the plan?" Jasek said, the illusion she thought he was in command fading with each word.

"We can't leave the portal undefended."

She looked at him, clearly wanting more.

"We'll defend it," he said. "Just from the other side. We'll set up camp and hope the sentinels keep doing their jobs long enough for us to find out what's going on. If we find that everything's okay, and we can get our supplies and replacement, there's a way back." He looked Private Chi in the eye. "And if necessary, you blow it."

Chi swallowed and looked away.

"You can blow it?"

"I already told you he could, Sir."

"With respect, Sergeant, I'd like to hear that from Private Chi."

She straightened. "Yes, Sir."

"I can, Sir," said Chi.

His authority was back—for now.

They left at midnight, Jasek steering from stern, Chi at the prow, and Rami and Keph sitting on the bench in the middle, all with rifles ready. When they neared the portal, Keph ordered blackout, and signaled to Jasek to kill the motor. They glided through the portal, slipping from a world overseen by a quarter-moon dimmed by swamp-gas to a clear night sky full of stars and the bright thumbnail of a silver moon overlooking New York Harbor.

They removed their helmets and breathed fresh, unfiltered air for the first time in fourteen months.

In the next moment, Keph absorbed several pieces of information in quick succession: above them, he caught a glimpse of a soaring creature with outspread wings, like a man wearing gliders and a mask with a freakishly long beak; then another creature crisscrossing the first's path in the air, and then another; then he saw Chi lift up his gun and, out of the corner of his eye, Rami do the same.

“Stop!” he whispered, putting a hand on the muzzle of Rami's rifle. “No one fire.” He turned quickly to make sure Jasek was lowering her gun too; for over a year, they'd honed the instinct to shoot anything that moved. He beckoned for Jasek and Chi to join them in the middle of the boat.

“They haven't noticed us yet,” he whispered. “But fire and you bring them all down on us.” The sky was full of the creatures.

“Are those pterodactyls?” Jasek whispered back.

Before he could answer, Chi said, “Lieutenant, did you ever hear of a Dinosaur Earth beyond any of the portals?”

“No. None of the portals led to a prehistoric Earth.”

“But them?” Chi said, pointing at the pterodactyls circling above.

“It looks like they opened a new portal,” Keph said.

The shoreline was a hundred feet away, but the current was bringing them toward it without the need to engage the motor. None of the circling pterodactyls appeared to have noticed them.

Peace treaty or no peace treaty, Keph thought, someone had made more bombs, and therefore, more portals.

He looked back at their portal. Above, the moon blinked out as an approaching pterodactyl uttered a drawn-out shriek.

“Lieutenant?” Chi said, raising his voice just above the whisper they'd been using. “Do you want me to...”

As if in response, the radio abruptly crackled to life.

“This is an emergency beacon,” it said. “Earth is no longer safe. Turn back if you can.”

They watched the circling pterodactyls as they listened to the message. War. New portals, hundreds of them. What had come through those portals... Command had fallen; Earth's cities destroyed. Humanity had been decimated.

The radio died out. A few moments later, it crackled to life again: “This is an emergency beacon. Earth is no longer safe. Turn back if you can.”

Jasek had placed her hand on Keph's shoulder while they waited for the flyer to pass. “We can’t stay here,” she whispered.

“We can't go back,” Keph said. “We'll take our chances here. Close the portal, Private Chi.”

Private Chi looked to Sergeant Jasek.

“Do it,” Keph said.

Chi nodded slowly and began typing commands on his armband. After a few moments, he looked up. “Sarge?”

“I gave you an order, Private.”

Jasek reached out a hand and shook her head.

“Early surveys show we can live there, beyond the swamp.” She looked up at the circling monsters. “We sure as hell can’t here.”

At that moment Keph felt command slip away. He had thought it would hurt. But it didn’t.

<<>>

“Come with us, Lieutenant.” Jasek spoke from the loaded boat, a second one crammed with every supply left in the Hold.

“I have a mission,” he said, and looked up at the explosives lining the ceiling. This time the portal had to be closed to protect from the creatures that had wiped out humanity on Real Earth. If only Chi’s remote control worked from this side... He pushed the thought away. “Now get out of here.” He saluted the tiny squad. “That’s an order.”

They returned his salute as one. He nodded, then shut the door. The burden of command was back on his shoulders.

Snapshots of Aleppo

Pedro Iniguez

The images still lingered in Santiago Serrano's head after he closed his eyes: the streaks on the wall of the market from the water balloons; the line of olive trees on the horizon standing tall along the powder-blue sky; the clay-colored roof of the school baking in the sun.

He opened his eyes. A grey plume of dust, ash, and smoke hung in the air. Across the way, the broken slabs from the collapsed market spat out mangled limbs. Rebar jutted out of the sides of the school walls like the splintered bones from the children's corpses underneath. Crimson runoff poured down the crumbled balcony of a house, cascading onto the street below.

The filthy air filled Santiago's lungs as he sucked in a deep breath. He coughed and looked around. The perch he was lying on was still intact. It was a flat piece of wall that had broken loose during the bombing run the month prior. He'd laid on it, holding his camera steady like a sniper, and lined up a perfect shot. In the frame, a rosy-cheeked child in a black Nike t-shirt and a pair of khaki shorts had trotted toward the school grounds. He wore a backpack too big for his body, probably stuffed with schoolbooks. The image reminded Santiago of a soldier sprinting through the streets with a large rucksack. Santiago adjusted the focus on the lens. His index finger had pressed the button as the explosion rocked the street like thunder in a closet.

Instinct had taken over. Santiago wrapped one arm around his eyes and, with the other, tucked the camera under his belly. When he opened his eyes the scene around him had morphed. One second to the next—another world.

Santiago lay motionless and listened for the sound of planes or bombs whistling from the sky. Nothing. Just the quiet of a snapshot frozen in time. His hand patted the ground, probing through the pebbles and fragments of cement. He felt the warm plastic of the camera's body and draped the strap around his neck as he pushed himself up. There was a buzzing in his ear, the vibrations ringing like a Theremin from the old black-and-white monster films he'd seen as a child.

Santiago hopped off his perch and landed two feet below on the street. He waved away a wisp of smoke. A mustached man standing by the entrance of the broken market gestured for Santiago to come over, mumbling under his breath. Santiago recognized the man as a vendor. He stood over the mangled corpse of a dead woman, every limb pointing in a different direction, like the hands of a compass on an antiquated map. A bounty of exploded fruit littered the street beside the woman's head.

"No," the man screamed. "This cannot be."

As Santiago knelt beside the woman, her eyes rolled back. A deep gash marked the side of her head.

"I'm sorry," Santiago said, lowering his head. "Was she your wife?"

"Look at my fruit," the man yelled. "They've ruined my fruit." The vendor dropped to his knees and scooped as many fruits as he could between his torso and his hands. "Do you think they will still buy these? They still taste good. I know it."

Santiago stood and stepped away from the vendor. "You're in shock. I'll go find help." The woman's head stirred slightly. Her eyes rolled sideways until they found Santiago.

"Don't bother with him," she said through gritted teeth. "He gets that way. Always overdramatizing everything. You should see how he gets when someone tries to haggle with him."

"Ma'am, are you alright?"

Before she answered, something tugged at Santiago's shirt. He looked down and saw the boy in the black Nike shirt. He wore a mask of ash and asbestos. The boy's chest gaped where the white swoosh used to be. A bloody set of exposed ribs protruded from the cavity, the bones looking as if slathered in barbecue sauce.

"Let her be," the boy said. "She needs to rest."

"My God," Santiago said. "You need to lie down. I'll go get help. There's an international medical station just a few miles from here."

"No. You don't understand. That's not the way this goes." The boy extended five chubby digits toward Santiago. "Come with me. I was on my way to school, but I think you're the one who needs teaching today."

"What the hell?"

"Don't be afraid. We're safe here. The moment has paused for us."

"I don't follow."

"Look at your watch."

Santiago lifted his hand. The hands on his watch lay idle.

"This must be a nightmare," Santiago said, shaking his wrist.

"Worse. This is life." The boy wrapped his hand around Santiago's middle and index finger and tugged. Santiago stepped forward as the boy led him through the smoking rubble, his backpack bouncing with every step.

"Where are we?" Santiago asked, lifting his camera.

"That won't work here. Nothing does. We are in the Levant. In Aleppo, Syria, exactly where you were during the bombing."

"Was it rebels? A terror cell? A drone strike?"

"It doesn't matter. Only the truth matters."

"And what is the truth?"

"What you see around you," the boy said sweeping a small hand over the chaos.

Across the street, a man sat on the driver's seat of a dilapidated yellow school bus. His hands still gripped the steering wheel, but the top of his head was caved inward so that his brains seeped out of his smiling mouth. Like a shredded tin can, the roof of the school bus swayed gently in a warm breeze.

Santiago turned away and gagged, swallowing back the hot current of vomit in his mouth.

"Have you been a photojournalist long?"

"This is my first international assignment."

"Where have you done most of your reporting?"

"I'm based out of Buenos Aires."

"And what about this scene troubles you?"

"Well, look at it. The death, the destruction." Santiago grabbed a tuft of his hair and pulled until his scalp burned.

"People die every day," the boy said with a smile.

"Yes, but this could have been avoided."

"How?"

Santiago said nothing.

"To you this is barbaric. You see the world through a single lens. The lens is shaped by your upbringing, your prejudices, and your privileges. Anything outside your worldview is alien and terrible. You are in one of the oldest cities in the world. War has always swept through this land like a tempest on an island or a volcano in the mountains. It is as natural a disaster as an earthquake or a flood."

"No, that's not true. War is man-made."

"And Man is of the Earth as much as the rains are."

"So, you're saying there's nothing that could have been done?"

"I never said that. There is a natural order to things. A hierarchy to the world. Once you understand that, real work can begin."

"A hierarchy?"

"Yes. I will show you." The boy squeezed Santiago's hand and led him toward the entrance of the collapsed school. A pile of concrete slabs and shattered walls created a small mountain over the steps of the building. There was a faint movement under the rubble.

"Help me move the debris," the boy said, pushing a five-foot piece of concrete slab with his small hands.

Santiago unslung the camera from his neck and set it on the ground. He squatted and pushed on a corner of the wall, shimmying it to the side. Under the slab, a boy and a girl squirmed, their lungs rising and falling like fish gasping their last breaths. Their shirts were soaked in deep crimson, permeating the air with the smell of copper.

"Those two," the boy said, "are royalty." He took a breath of his own, the tatters of his shirt shifting with the air that passed through his torso.

"Royalty?"

"Children are the kings and queens of this world. They must be protected at all costs, lest we lose our way. Without them and their guidance, we live blind, pointless lives. Their pure hearts and innocent minds represent the truest sense of mankind, the best of what we can be. Today, there are many kings and queens under all the rubble."

"This is too much. I need a glass of water." Santiago took two paces away from the school and sat on the street so that he faced the other end of the block. Smoke rose into the sky over homes toppled like spilled dominoes. A few scattered palm trees burned like torches.

"Who could do this?" Santiago asked. "Monsters."

"The soldiers that did this are the court artists. They were paid to create this. Some believe in the art, others don't. It's just their job. If you ask me," the boy said, scanning the city, "the carnage reminds me of modern surrealist sculptures. Don't you think so?"

"You think there's beauty here?"

"I only comment on what is. You take pictures of chaos for a living. Don't you look for the beauty in the shot? The glory of the composition?"

"I only observe. I try to capture the truth of the moment."

"Then you don't need a camera for that. If you want the root of the truth, look over there." The boy pointed. On the horizon, a square of office buildings stood higher than the surrounding sand-colored structures. "That is where the politicians gather. That is where they squabble like wild birds and make a mockery of life. They are the court jesters of the world. Their laws, their wars, it's all one big joke. Somewhere down the line they grasped power away from the children. The jesters run the world now."

"How did they grasp power?"

"The citizens, the peasants, the guardians of the children either voted for them, or were afraid to challenge the fiery rhetoric of monarchs who came and went. But that is too long of a story and we are short on time."

"Why are you telling me this?"

"Because everyone has a part to play. Even you."

Santiago stood. "How? What can I do?"

"The world will continue as it always does. Few notice the squabbles of a lonely city perched on a rock amidst the olive trees. You can make them aware of our plight. There has to be an uproar. Perhaps you can influence a king or a queen today, so that tomorrow they will not grow to be jesters."

Santiago took a deep breath and looked at the destruction around him. "Tell me what to do."

"You will be the courier that sends the message. Simply go back to your perch as you were, and the rest will take care of itself."

"That's it?"

"That's it. Now go, I have to take up my position as well. Hurry before the moment is lost."

Santiago snatched his camera and paced back to his spot. He climbed the perch and lay flat on his belly exactly as he had before the bombs detonated. He looked back at the boy, now lying motionless on the street. A breeze blew through his hair and made clouds of dust like powdered sugar. The woman by the market ceased to stir, as the merchant stared at his exploded fruit in anguish. The rubble by the school remained in a still cloud of smoke.

Santiago lifted the camera and looked through the viewfinder. He shifted the lens and zoomed out, capturing the wide scene of chaos in front of him. The dead would have a messenger today. Their story would be told. If he could do this much, he'd be happy.

Before he snapped the shot, Santiago felt a peculiar tightness in his chest. His fingers probed down his shirt until he felt the jagged pieces of metal protruding from his heart. He coughed and spit out a small spray of blood. As he tilted his head, blood spewed from his torso, running down the perch and mixing with the blood of the children and the oil streaks on the street. Santiago looked at his watch. The small hands ticked forward again. He laid his head down, feeling the warm touch of sun-kissed concrete. Before he closed his eyes, he heard the familiar snap of a camera behind him.

"Fuck," he heard someone say. "Look at all the blood. This shot's making the front page."

Santiago smiled as he closed his eyes, and the ghosts of Aleppo greeted him as one of their own.

Portraits from the Shadow

D. Thomas Minton

When Trung disembarked at LAX, the dead began whispering to him. In the underground tunnel connecting the international terminal to the domestic one, the spirit of a young woman whimpered from the murky shadows. He tried to console her, but only managed to attract the attention of a uniformed man who told him to move along. In Denver, the ghost of an angry teen hissed at him as he stepped off the rental car shuttle. All along the lonely road twisting up through the forest of snow-capped pines, lost spirits glared at him from the edge of the blacktop. America, like Vietnam, had a problem with ghosts.

Trung was thankful when he arrived at Hampton McElvy's cabin and found no spirits haunting it. His fingers ached as he released the steering wheel and sat quietly, trying to collect himself. He had traveled halfway around the world to speak with McElvy. What if the man couldn't help him? Trung wasn't sure he could handle another disappointment.

He touched the pocket of his jacket. The crinkle of the paper within reassured him. Trung dismissed thoughts of failure.

After several deep breaths, he climbed onto the porch and rapped quietly on the plank door. The hinges creaked; an eye squinted out through the narrow crack.

"I don't give interviews anymore," McElvy said, his drawl sounding like John Wayne. To Trung, every American sounded like John Wayne.

The door started to close.

“No interview,” Trung said, putting his hand against the wood. He removed the yellowed rectangle of newsprint from his pocket and held it up for McElvy to see.

“I don't talk about that anymore,” McElvy said.

“Please, I came from Vietnam to speak to you.”

The eye blinked at him.

“I am hopeful you can tell me about this man,” Trung said. “He is my father.”

<<>>

Trung set the clipping on the table between them. Three weeks ago, he had found it among his mother's things after her funeral. Trung had never seen a picture of his father before, but his uncle had confirmed the identity of the man in the newspaper photo.

McElvy studied his knuckles as his knobby fingers worked them over. Life had taken a knife to his face and carved fissures around his eyes and across his forehead. “Ask what you need to ask,” he said.

Even with the wood fire in the stove, a chill clung to the room.

“My name is Nguyễn Hiếu Trung. I am from Vietnam. For twenty years I have searched for my father's spirit so I can bring it home, but I cannot find him. Do you remember this man?”

The way McElvy's mouth twitched, it looked to Trung like he was having a conversation with himself.

Trung shifted in the wooden chair. He thought about the money he had spent to get there and was starting to regret his decision. Impulsive and wasteful, he chided himself. Maybe his uncle had been right after all. Why would an American remember a single North Vietnamese soldier he had photographed over forty years ago?

“I remember 'em all,” McElvy said, his voice barely audible. “They don't let me forget...”

<<>>

In January of '68, I volunteered to go to Vietnam as a stringer for the Associated Press. If you wanted to make a name for yourself, that's what you did. I was fresh off the tarmac when the North launched the Tet Offensive. They took the ancient city of Huế, about fifteen miles north of where I was housed with the 5th Marines.

Huế was crawling with NVA. Bullets and bombs. Booby traps everywhere, and not the kind that killed you fast, but the kind that took off a foot or a hand or cut you deep enough that you'd bleed to death 'cause they couldn't get choppers in with all the heat.

I spent two weeks thinking I'd never see another day. I slept next to bodies, with their stink for a blanket. When I ate my rations, I ate death. At night, we'd hole-up in some dark building, and we'd hear screaming and groaning outside. Sometimes in English, sometimes not. Nothing we could do. We learned that lesson quick, when a Marine tried to help a little boy burned by napalm. He took a bullet in the neck and screamed until he finally died. Seemed like it took an hour, but couldn't have been more than a minute. We couldn't get to him; all we could do was watch and listen, listen to him gurgling and weeping, as he bled into his lungs.

Lance Corporal Stillman. Nineteen. He had a girl back in Omaha and a baby on the way who would never see his daddy.

<<>>

McElvy's Adam's apple slid up and down his long throat like a yoyo on a string. “You can't learn to survive something like Huế,” he said. “It was sheer dumb-ass luck who came home and who didn't.”

Outside, the day darkened as snow began to fall. The yellow light from the overhead bulb huddled around the two men, as if it was afraid to venture into the room's darkening corners.

“We lost a lot of good people over there, but then, so did you.”

Every person Trung knew had lost family members in the war: fathers, mothers, brothers, sisters, millions of Vietnamese people. Many of them had never been found or properly buried, leaving their ghosts trapped in the shadow between the pain of the living and the peace of the afterlife. As long as their loved ones were lost, the living had failed their ancestors and would not prosper.

Trung had devoted his life to using his gift to reunite families with their lost dead, or just as often, the dead with their lost families. Yet, after years of searching, he had never been able to find the one ghost he truly needed to.

McElvy's bloodless-white knuckles gripped the edge of the table. “In Huế, I was sure death was looking for me,” he said. “I couldn't have been more right and more wrong.”

<<>>

The day after Stillman died, we got lit up by the NVA. In that craziness, I got separated, which is not a good place to be with nothing but a Nikon F. Not knowing what else to do, I ran. No care for how or where.

I ran until I got my wits back enough to realize running like that would do nothing but get me killed. I ducked into a building that at least had walls and a roof. I found a dark corner and sat there and shook and shook. Couldn't stop myself.

About that time is when I saw him. He came in through a doorway from another room. A Marine, young, face smeared with dirt and paint, all quiet like. He squatted next to me, leaned on his rifle like it was a walking stick, and that's when I recognized him.

I thought I was hallucinating or maybe it was his brother. I didn't know. I said, “Is that you Stillman? You okay?”

He had this look on his face, serene, like the world no longer mattered to him, like he was beyond it all, aloof. Yet I could see a sadness in the tilt of his eyes and the way he looked past me, like watching something faraway, something wonderful that he could never get to.

I touched his arm to get his attention. It was cold, unnaturally cold, and my stomach dropped out of me like I fell out of an airplane.

I did then what I was trained to do. I took his picture. I shot his face wide open at a thousandth, because of the light. Soft on the edges, but the eyes were sharp enough to see right into his soul. Right in, like lookin' down a well. Then he stood up.

I hissed at him to stay down or Charlie might see him, but he didn't need to worry about that anymore. He paused at the doorway he'd come out of and motioned for me to come with him. Then he was gone.

<<>>

McElvy's mouth worked like he was chewing a piece of gristle. “I saw Stillman die, but there he was.”

Realizing he hadn't been breathing, Trung drew a sharp breath. He couldn't decide if McElvy was telling the truth or if the stress of combat had caused him to see things. Vietnam was full of spirit mediums who claimed to have the gift to commune with the dead, but in Trung's experience, few people had the true gift to do that. Most were charlatans taking advantage of people's need for closure. “In Vietnam, we believe the dead can haunt the living. They can be helpful or they can hurt you. Vietnam is land of ghosts, many from the War with America, and we cannot forget the lost ones. To do so dishonors them and dishonors us.”

McElvy looked up from his hands with weary eyes.

The room seemed cold enough to crystallize the old man's breath, but only words came out of his mouth.

<<>>

After Stillman went through that door, I sat there for a long time trying to figure out if I was hallucinating. It crossed my mind that maybe I was already dead, and to be honest, to this day I don't know if I am or not.

But I was a photographer, a journalist, and my curiosity wouldn't let me be.

As I neared the doorway, I heard a droning sound. Some light came in through a hole on that side of the building, so I could see into the other room. It was filled with flies, everywhere, like a cloud of black pebbles. The biggest flies I've ever seen, but then, with all them bodies, what did I expect?

Must have been two, three hundred of 'em, laying on the ground like they were knocked over bowling pins. Women still clutching little kids, old men with their hands tied behind their backs. Many of them gaped up at me appalled, like I'd crashed some private party. They was all shot in the back of the head, execution style.

I just stood there, looking, 'cause I didn't know what else to do, and that's when I saw her. A young woman, movie-star beautiful. Sitting there with no expression I could read on her face, sort of as if she had no opinion one way or the other about what had happened. She looked through me, with eyes like Stillman's—faraway. The pupils big, so I could see right into them. I could see flashes of who she was, her life, like little vignettes played out with shadow puppets.

My hands were shaking so much, I could barely lift my camera, but when I got it up to my eye, everything just changed. My hands went rock-steady. Without thought, they worked my Nikon's settings; f/16 at a thirtieth, because I wanted to see every strand of dark hair as it framed her face. I shot only one picture; then she got up and left. As she did, an old man sat down in her place. I shot him from slightly above, f/4 at one-five hundredth, so his face would rise up out of the bodies beneath him.

More came. Kids with their mothers, men not fit to fight, more woman, some beautiful, some not. I never changed film; it never occurred to me. I just kept shooting and shooting and shooting, picture after picture, and then they'd get up and leave and go someplace I-don't-know-where because someone else always sat down. I took pictures until it got too dark.

Then everything got quiet. No flies, no explosions, no screams. Just quiet.

For the first time since entering Huế, I felt at peace.

I sat in that room all night, so dark I could see nothing. The stink must have been incredible, but the whole damn city stank, so I didn't notice.

I saw him with the first light. Where he came from, I don't know. He sat among the bodies, like a heron in a rice paddy. Sat there, perfectly still. He wore a NVA uniform, and scared me so much I nearly pissed myself. But then I saw his face, and I knew I had nothing to fear. I saw what looked like regret, maybe for things done, or maybe not done.

We sat like that until the dawn moved across the floor and put light on him. Then I took his picture. It was the last one I remember taking.

<<>>

McElvy held the yellowed newsprint in his trembling hands. "I photographed your daddy wide open at a thirtieth.

It never should have come out," he said, "but he wouldn't be denied."

Trung's body thrummed. If he could find the building, maybe he could find his father's spirit, not to mention the hundreds of others that likely still haunted that killing ground. "Where was this place?"

McElvy shrugged.

Trung's face flushed hot. How could McElvy dismiss his question? Trung restrained himself from raising his voice. He was in McElvy's home, and as an American, McElvy could not understand the importance of bringing lost spirits home. Trung lowered his eyes as he tried to balance his challenge with a show of respect. "You must help me find that building."

"It wasn't far from the place they call the Citadel, but I can't say more. Getting there was crazy. Getting out, I was crazy. A group from the 5th Marines found me seven days later, still sittin' there. They heard my camera clicking, and pried it out of my hands, so I was told some days later. I don't remember any of it after that first night. Finding that building doesn't matter, though, because he ain't there. None of them are there anymore."

Trung exhaled a sharp breath. He closed his eyes and concentrated on slowing his pulse. What did this American know? It didn't matter that the bodies were no longer there; the bodies were not important.

McElvy grabbed Trung's wrist; his cold fingers sucked away any warmth remaining in Trung's arm. "He ain't there." McElvy's eyes had a wild gleam to them.

Trung pulled his arm away. His chair scrapped back several inches with the sudden motion. He had seen that same glint in the eyes of some of the Vietnamese veterans, the ones who hadn't been able to leave the war behind.

"There ain't no rhyme or reason," McElvy said. "Why does one man die when his buddy next him lives? What makes good men do bad things?" McElvy rose. In the sepia halo of light, he seemed much taller than Trung remembered. "You came all this way to find your daddy, didn't you?" He retreated into the shadows lingering at the room's perimeter. He stopped at a door that Trung had not noticed before.

McElvy tugged at the bolt with his knobby fingers until it gave.

Trung rose and backed away. “What's in there?”

McElvy pulled the door aside. The opening was a black rectangle etched on the darkness. Without answering, McElvy stepped through the doorway and was gone.

Silence settled on the room like a snowfall. Trung hugged his arms and shivered. Out the window, snow collected on the windshield of his rental car. At the rate it was sticking, the road would soon be impassible, and he would be trapped here. Trung became uncomfortably aware of how little he knew about McElvy or his prejudices.

Trung picked up the newspaper clipping and stuffed it into his pocket. McElvy had admitted that he had nothing else he could tell him about the whereabouts of his father. If he left now, he could at least get back to a road that might still be clear of snow. Yet, Trung had crossed the world to learn everything he could about his father. Was there anything else McElvy could tell him? If there was anything more, no matter how small, he could not leave.

Trung stopped at the doorway through which McElvy had disappeared. Cold air, like that from a meat locker, blew out the opening and sent a violent shiver through his entire body. After several long seconds, his eyes adjusted to the dimness of the narrow room, its windows covered with thick oil cloths to block out the light.

McElvy stood before a bank of file cabinets. The mist from his breath swirled around his head as he spoke.

<<>>

I spent a month in a hospital in Saigon; then I left Vietnam. I gave my film to the AP, and told them I was done. When I got home, I put my camera in a box and tried to go about my life, but you don't just go back to life after that. You don’t just shower away that kind of filth.

I started hearing voices, soldiers, woman, crying babies, English and Vietnamese and God knows what else. I thought I was going crazy. They were coming from my closet. When I opened the door, I would hear them like they were hiding in the pockets of my shirts. I pulled my closet apart, looking everywhere for them. My shoes. The pockets of my pants. The boxes of junk. Then I found my Nikon. The voices were coming out of it. I opened the back and inside was a roll of film.

I'm sure I gave the AP all my film, every last bloody roll of it. Yet there it was, and as I held it in my hands, I could hear the voices so loud in my head, all talking at me so I couldn't separate any single one, like I was in a huge crowd, and all of them were clamoring for my attention.

I cleared off my dark room and developed the roll, but the film was blank, until I started making prints. Then I saw the faces. The first one was Lance Corporal Stillman. When I touched his print, I heard his voice in my head, clear as if he was standing next me and speaking into my ear. He told me about how much he missed his wife, and how sorry he was that he would never see his baby grow up. He begged me to find them and tell them that he loved them. He begged me to take him home.

I promised him I would.

I printed photo after photo, hundreds of 'em, all from that blank roll of film. Each portrait spoke to me as I printed it and hung it to dry. There were more faces than I remembered from that room, there were soldiers, both American and Vietnamese, more civilians, more children, more women and men. Hundreds upon hundreds like everyone who died at Huế had lined up for their portrait.

Sometimes they asked me to find their parents or husbands or wives. Sometimes they begged me to tell their story. Sometimes they just cried, and I couldn't understand what they wanted. Most I couldn't understand, 'cause I don't speak Vietnamese.

I kept my promise to Stillman. It took me months to find his widow. When I told her why I was there, she slapped me across the face and slammed the door on me. I slipped the portrait underneath. As I let it go, I felt Stillman's presence leave in peace. He was home, and he seemed to know it.

As I walked away, the door opened, and she stood there, tears on her face, holding my picture in one hand, Stillman's baby in the other. She didn't say anything to me, but I could see everything I needed to see in her eyes.

<<>>

McElvy pulled open a drawer of the file cabinet. Stuffed inside were old manila envelopes.

Trung came forward, as if reeled into the dark room by a string. He felt an energy emanating from the drawer. At first it rose up from the tattered envelopes like a murmur, but as he drew nearer, it grew louder, like a crowd awakening from a long sleep. In the noise, Trung heard voices, jumbled together like noodles.

"I tried to find them all," McElvy said, "but I didn't even know where to start. In '76, I went back to Saigon—Hồ Chí Mihn City—not an easy thing to do at that time. With the help of a Vietnamese art dealer, I hung pictures in some galleries, hoping someone would recognize them, hoping someone would hear something and believe me. Your daddy's picture was one of them. But I got nothing."

Trung's hand hovered over the envelopes. Goosebumps rose on the back. Without thought, he reached into the drawer and pulled out an envelope. It took both hands to work it free.

"I took good care of them," McElvy said, "as well as I could, but they want to go home. They need to go home."

Trung's fingers shook so much he had difficulty unwinding the thread that held the flap closed. He slid a glossy print halfway out. His father's eyes, stared at him. He looked younger than he ever imagined.

"I—" Trung's voice cracked in his throat. He pressed the photograph against his cheek, unable to speak. The picture smelled of mildew and age, but it was warm against his skin, like a parent's comforting hand. Trung closed his eyes and imagined what his life would have been like with his father. His uncle had done as well as he could, but sometimes a boy simply needed his father.

"It's me; it's Trung," he whispered in Vietnamese.

"I'm sorry," his father said gently into his ear.

Trung held the picture out and looked again into the eyes. They were crisp and clear, the edges pulled with sadness.

"If only I had obeyed, I would have been there for you," his father said.

In his father's eyes, Trung saw the room in Huế, the hundreds of unarmed people kneeling with their backs to a line of Vietnamese soldiers. Over the crying children and woman, a Vietnamese officer screamed at the soldiers to rid Vietnam of the imperialist sympathizers. When the soldiers hesitated, the officer drew his pistol and shot the soldier nearest him who had lowered his rifle. As the bullet ripped through his father's head, the line of rifles popped and rattled.

Trung screamed out, the picture crumpling in his hand. He pressed it to his forehead and wept.

<<>>

The photo in Trung's shirt pocket warmed his chest as he loaded the last of the sealed boxes into the back of the rental car. As he let go of it, the voices faded but did not go away.

Trung turned to McElvy standing in the snow to the side. He bowed to the old man. "I owe you—"

McElvy took his hand. "No," he said, and pressed a wad of green bills into Trung's palm. "To help."

Trung looked at the money. He had done nothing to deserve it, but to give it back would be an insult. He would earn the money then, he decided. "I will find their families," Trung said, knowing it was what McElvy needed to hear.

The lines around the old man's eyes softened.

As Trung pulled out onto the snowy road, the murmuring in the back of the car grew animated. The dead knew their journey home had finally begun.

Lanterne Rouge

Jeremy Thackray

This story is based on a true exploit.

AN EASTER FESTIVAL OF SPORT

Let us simply announce that all sportsmen...aviators, cyclists, automobilists, footballers, boxers...all without exception will be interested in a series of events including a Tour of the Battlefields which will pass through the whole of Alsace, the whole of Lorraine, through martyred Belgium, through all those places whose chains have been broken by Victory.

-Le Petit Journal, December 1918

<<>>

Stage #1-Strasbourg-Luxembourg, 275km

April 28, 1919, 06.00hrs

Louis Ellner, a nobody, is about to begin the Circuit des Champs de Bataille: the toughest bicycle race in history. He is going to lose. He will do so by a cavernous margin. He will claim no glory and no infamy. He is going to break his body and quite possibly his mind in order to be totally forgotten.

Louis knows all this. He's entered anyway.

At the start line in Strasbourg's Place Broglie, he grins. It is an expression beyond his control, lunatic in its width. His teeth chatter in the brisk spring wind. The cream of professional cycling—or what's left of it, after—sit astride their steeds in front of him, stoking on cigarettes and coffee thick as tar. Alavoine, Duboc, Deruyter, Van Lerberghe, Neffati: the fastest and hardest of the remnant peloton. Their bicycles are gleaming, chains oiled, bars freshly taped.

Louis's bike, a De Dion Bouton Routier, is possibly the same one he was riding in 1914, depending on your definition—he cannot recall if he has changed every last component since then, or almost every last one.

His woollen jersey is patched at the left elbow. He made his own leg warmers, badly.

His knees knock.

He does not mind, for he is here.

Despite the early start, a crowd of thousands, from ragged peasants to the top-hatted gentry, has gathered to see them off. Scores of boys in caps and smocks coo over the professionals' machines, armies of bakers and sausage-sellers drum up much-needed business, and a band oompahs *La Marseillaise*.

Only Louis sees Madame Tricolore.

She stands in the centre of the road, a towering image of France, the red-white-blue made statuesque. She is made of the flag: its fabric flows about her like the most silken of dresses, but it is also her skin, the stitching her veins. When she speaks her voice is that of Jeanne D'Arc, or Delacroix's Liberty, or any other fancy of the patriot in Louis's soul. Her tripartite radiance fills this Strasbourg square.

"*Pour la France, mes amis*!" she cries. "My brave, brave men! Honour the fallen, and may your road be fair! *Allez, allez*!"

The starter pistol is raised—fired!—and Louis's toil begins.

The professionals are away like bullets, and he hammers the pedals merely to keep in touch. Madame Tricolore, now floating on the wind, keeps pace and exhorts them with song—"*Bonne chance! Bonne chance! Pour l'honneur, pour la France!*"

It does not help Louis. Within twenty kilometres the peloton splits, a straggling grupetto drifting to the rear. Within forty kilometres he is alone in last place: the race's *lanterne rouge*.

Madame Tricolore pays heed to the man from Épernay, flying silently alongside Louis. Her form changes with the landscape of Alsace. Sometimes she is a dove with red and blue wings. Sometimes she is the wind itself, her shape and colours just visible in the corners of Louis's eye. Once, as he races down an avenue of elms, the leaves turn blue-white-red at his passing.

After one hundred kilometres, she speaks. "Louis, my brave boy, you struggle so! I am honoured."

He answers between panting breaths. "It is my pleasure, madame."

"The riders ahead have reached half-way. They will slow the pace at Metz—push on and you will have them!"

"Madame…"

"Do it for my honour, dear son of my soil!"

"Madame…I will not catch them…and I am not here for you."

Madame Tricolore's red flares redder than blood. Louis grinds out rotations.

"This race is in my honour," says Tricolore. Her voice has less passion, but more sincerity. "To bring back my colour after years of brown and grey. What else can you be here for?"

Louis would shrug if his shoulders weren't so stiff. "You have seven stages to find out," he says. "My apologies, Madame."

He puts his head down and powers on. When he next looks up, Tricolore is gone.

The stage is awful. The roads are rutted, the rain hammers down, and by the time he arrives in Luxembourg, shaking with bone-deep exhaustion after nineteen hours in the saddle, the rest of the riders are in bed.

But he has not abandoned the race, as some have.

In the few seconds between his head striking a pillow and deep, deep sleep enveloping him, he hears a whisper on the wind.

"*Adieu*, Louis. But I will find out. *Allez, allez...*"

General Classification after Stage 1

1. Egg, Oscar (Sui)-10hr 58min

71. Ellner, Louis (Fra)-+7hr 52min

Stage #2-Luxembourg-Bruxelles, 301km

April 30, 1919, 05.00hrs

Louis does not enjoy his day's rest. It is a functional thing; spent in massaging the legs, inspecting his bike, readying his bags and his bidons. It goes all too quickly.

The peloton cruises out of Luxembourg the next morning at a milder pace. For a moment Louis wonders if the cruelty of Stage 1 has cowed the leaders' enthusiasm. Not so: at the 10km mark, the Belgian armada attacks, drawing the rest of the peloton with them. Louis is soon returned to last place.

Skirting the ruined forts of Liege, he is stunned as a fine figure on a sparkling bicycle, mud-free and polished, sweeps past him. Louis catches a glimpse of a face alight with competitive fire and a moustache waxed to a gleam. Everything about him speaks of a mighty champion, but, to Louis's further surprise, this champion does not gallop away. Instead, he commands:

"Stay in my wheel, monsieur!"

It is a voice that could have led the line at Verdun. Louis obeys—

and flies! Their pace ascends until Louis is certain that he will be dropped, but he sticks to the Champion's wheel like mud to a *poilu's* boot. Their chains whirl, their tyres hum, and they skim on the potholed macadam roads as if they were paved with lacquered teak. They must be at thirty, thirty-five, forty kilometres an hour! It is a miracle!

Of course, it's not, and he knows it, but Louis thrills at the sensation anyway.

After an hour of joyous labour, the Champion peels away from the front and pedals at Louis's side. "Fine riding, monsieur! We shall make a hero of you yet."

"But the newspaper said all entrants would be heroes," says Louis.

"Ha! Of course. Heroes, they are of different qualities, and heroism takes many forms."

Louis beholds a slow transformation. He does not see any one part of the Champion's body, clothing, or bicycle change, but each time he looks something has shifted. His bike has parts that Louis does not recognise: are those more gears mounted on his back wheel, rather than just the two that Louis has? Is that a lever with which the Champion can change gear without getting off? And the colours of his jersey are brighter now, the cut more fitted to his form.

"Monsieur," says the Champion. "Let me tell you why I am here: to guess why *you* are here."

"Ah," says Louis. "Did Madame send you?"

"*Oui*. But I know, monsieur. I *know*. An athlete like you, I can see it, where Madame Tricolore could not."

The Champion changes again. His cap and moustache are gone and his hair is slicked aggressively back. His bike looks lighter and stiffer. Random words emblazon his jersey.

"You are here," says the Champion, "For the challenge. For the test. To know your strength, to better yourself, and if to better others, so much the better! To measure yourself against wind and rain and road. That is the sweetest thing in life for a sportsman!"

Louis considers. He is a fine amateur. He enjoys the test, certainly. But *this* test? *This* race? There are saner ways to test oneself than by riding over 'roads' filled with unexploded shells, only six months after he himself fought upon them.

"No," says Louis. "I don't think that is it."

The Champion smirks. A wire on his neck trails to a device in his ear, and his bike looks like something from a Jules Verne novel. "Nonsense! Of course, that is it."

Louis shrugs. Pain creeps back into his muscles and he draws deeper breaths. "No," he repeats. "I can test myself back home. That is not why I am here. My apologies, monsieur."

The Champion does not look convinced, not that Louis can see his eyes anymore. His companion wears a visored helmet and is wrapped in a skin-tight blue suit. His forearms are tucked together on specialist handlebars. He looks like an arrow in flight.

“Well,” says the Champion, “I respect you, monsieur, but you may change your mind yet.”

The Champion blasts off at an impossible pace. The further away he gets, the more the cold bites at Louis’s skin. When he is out of sight, Louis pulls over, vomits, gets back on, and makes his weary way onward to Brussels.

“No, I won’t,” he mutters, perhaps to himself.

<u>General Classification after Stage 2</u>

1. Dejonghe, Albert (Bel) -23hr 23min

51. Ellner, Louis (Fra)-+16hr 29min

Stage #3—Bruxelles-Amiens, 323km

May 2, 1919, 04.30hrs

Stages 1 and 2 were, in hindsight, purgatory. Stage 3 is straight to the ninth *cercle de l'Enfer.*

There are no roads, only mud. There is no light, only a dead grey un-dark. There is no clear air, only howling wind soaked in freezing, bitter water. The race is crossing the Zone Rouge, an area so blasted by artillery and its soil so sickly with chlorine and lead that surely it will be cursed for a century to come. The race has moved from the ridiculous to the outright cruel. A man could die competing here.

Louis won't, but not through lack of trying.

After thirty kilometres, the race splits front to back, but also side to side: the 'route' is so nebulous that riders are choosing different paths at each lonely, shell-shredded signpost, convinced they know the faster way.

Louis, content to reach the checkpoint when he reaches it, comes to a halt as the road (such as it is) ends.

He is alone in a wasteland. The wind slaps him repeatedly across the cheek like a drummer on a snare and it carries the whispers of the dead. He weeps. It is a necessary thing, not so unusual after any hundred kilometres in the wet, never mind this hundred. Cycling is an odd sport.

Seeing no clear way, he shoulders his bike and walks cross-country.

He sees the shattered frame of a building in the distance. Only when fifty metres away does he recognise it as a church. He passes it and becomes aware that a figure has followed him from the graveyard.

It is a man in a hooded brown robe, knotted with a cord at the waist. His beard is long and grey. He walks so, achingly, slowly, but somehow keeps pace with Louis despite the racer's relative hurry.

"Ah, my son," he says, his voice like a chapel bell. "You find me at last. I knew you would come."

Louis turns, seeing the greenery in the Hermit's unkempt beard and the mud on the hem of his robe. "Thank you, *Abbé*. Let me guess—Madame sent for you."

"And the Champion," says the Hermit. "You are doing God's work here, and ours."

Louis stumbles in a puddle, dunking his leg to the shin. "God's work is *very* hard today."

"Yes. But that is why you are here." The Hermit draws close. His breath smells of sodden earth; not only with water, but with chemicals, with detritus, with gas and with pestilence. "You are here for the sanctity of suffering. For the holiness of the struggle. The Champion saw something similar, but for him it is the glory of it. You, my son, are not here for glory. You are here to punish yourself as Christ did, as France did, and to redeem yourself of your sins. It is the cleansing fire you seek."

Louis chews his lip. There's something in what the Hermit says. Cycling *is* suffering, forcing the rider to dig deeper and deeper past every stratum of pain to a bedrock of courage. He loves to free-wheel down the hills of Épernay, but only once he's dragged himself up them in the first place. That's the point.

But these are not the hills of Épernay. These are the gored murder-fields of the Somme. He is covered head to toe in mud, can barely carry his bike, and still has some 160 km remaining. He should abandon now for his own safety.

"It's not the suffering I came for," he says, looking down at his exhausted body and gasping at the pain in his neck as he does so. "And it's not the suffering keeping me here. I'm not that much of a masochist."

"God knows otherwise," says the Hermit, "As will you, when your race comes to its end and you feel the purity of his grace. *Dies iræ, dies illa, dies tribulationis et angustiæ...*"

That night, Louis does not make it to the finish line. He stumbles upon a dugout long since abandoned by Tommies and falls to sleep amongst their ghosts. He finishes the stage the next day, 36 hours after he started it.

But he finishes the stage.

He finishes the stage.

<u>General Classification after Stage 3</u>

1. Deruyter, Charles (Bel)-43hr 09min

28. Ellner, Louis (Fra)-+32hr 01min

Stage #4-Amiens-Paris, 277km

May 4, 1919, 06.00hrs

Louis is a ruin of a man. Dirt seems ingrained in his skin; he secretes it. When he signs on for the beginning of Stage 4, the professionals are astonished. They have food, wine, and lodgings paid for by their teams, and even they are close to exhaustion. This Ellner, a mere *isolé*, has nothing but what he can scrounge. It shows.

He has missed the rest day, having only finished Stage 3 thirteen hours earlier. In any normal race he would have been disqualified, but the commissaires have removed the time cut. Had it remained, they would have had to cull half the pack, and there are few enough of them left as it is.

After their suffering on the Somme, there is agreement in the peloton that they will ride *piano* for the first part of the stage. No one attacks. Every man, from the leader down, aches. Some have amphetamines to dull the pain, but nothing can wipe it out.

Louis clings on at the back; *piano* for a professional is *forte* for him. Punctures and potholes thin the field. Early in the stage- he witnesses a rider do the bottlenose dolphin over the handlebars as his front wheel hits a shell-hole. Five hundred metres later he falls off himself, and the peloton is gone.

He is heading south towards Paris and less ravaged territory, but here, around St Quentin, Chauny, and Soissons, the conditions are no better than yesterday. Burned-out tanks litter the fields. Burial details still search for the corpses of the dead. A bomb explodes half a mile away, but Louis has become used to the sound. There are millions of shells for the army to clear.

This time Louis cries *on* the bike, not off it. It has nothing to do with the pain in his legs and chest and everything to do with the last four years. At the first checkpoint, already two hours down, he supresses his tears so the commissaires will not see him cry. When he departs the little café, the tears return.

As night begins to rust the leaden sky, he hears a scraping and a screeching at the roadside. Metal grinds on metal, girder on girder, and a monster of iron and ash erupts from the earth. He is a giant made of artillery, rifles, the bones of dead horses and the timbers of shattered trenches. His hair is scraps of soiled uniforms and barbed wire. The blood dripping from his face is mud.

Louis shrieks and sprints away, then slows: the Giant is not chasing him. The creature screeches as it walks, sparks flying from its grinding limbs, but its head is slumped into its chest and its arms loll like a monkey's. It limps, drawing one mangled foot through the earth like a broken plough, but its every stride is still ten feet, and it keeps pace at Louis's side.

The rider waits for an introduction. None comes.

"Monsieur," braves Louis, "Did Madame send you also?"

There is a rending deep in the Giant's throat. "Yeesss. She did." His vowels are like the thunder of a cannonade twenty miles off, and his consonants like the same close at hand. His syllables detonate. "Are you afraid of me?"

"It seems right to be afraid of you."

"Yeeess. You are, not, wrong."

A gunshot sounds somewhere nearby. Louis does not blink.

"You have something to tell me, I think," he says.

"I do," says the Giant, looking at Louis. Its eyes are two mismatched sniper scopes. "You came to this race to suffer."

"That was the Hermit's guess too. And the Champion's."

"No. You are not here to suffer *for* anything. Just to suffer. To loathe life. Loathe yourself. Loathe the world that birthed this scene and killed millions to do so. You came here because you lived where others did not. You seek a kind of death."

Oh, *this* comes close.

But...the people at the start lines each day. The life, returning. There were wars before and will be wars again, but between them still, is life. There is more to this than despair.

"You have something there, Monsieur," says Louis, wiping his streaming nose. "But not all of it. There is *something* at the end of my road."

"Can you say what?" says the Giant.

"No," Louis shrugs. "But it is there—I know it."

"Ahhhhhhhhhh," says the Giant, in a great exhalation like the drifting of gas in the wind. His fabric hair sheds, his tree-stump kneecaps hit the earth, and his gunwheel hips roll away. His scope-eyes fall from his skull, his pistol-fingers from his hands. The Giant is subsumed in the earth.

Louis enters Paris. The other riders finished the stage in the Parc des Princes velodrome, cheered on by 20,000 spectators. It is closed when he arrives. He makes his way to the night checkpoint and signs in. The commissaires knew to stay awake for him. He is gaining a reputation.

That night, he sobs into his blanket. The next morning his cheek and his pillow are still damp.

<u>General Classification after Stage 4</u>

1. Deruyter, Charles (Bel)-55hr 06min

24. Ellner, Louis (Fra)-+40hr 09min

Stage #5-Paris-Bar-le-Duc, 333km

May 7, 1919, 00.00hrs

Champagne! A reception is held at the offices of *Le Petit Journal on* the rest day. Louis feels somewhat out of place. This is a place for men like Jean Alavoine, currently residing in sixth place. He is a hero to Louis, a six-time Tour de France stage winner and conqueror of the Alps and Pyrenees. When Louis shakes his hand and hears Alavoine's admiration for him, he wonders if this is not why he is here: to collect stardust.

A midnight start to Stage 5 squashes that idea. This is an immense stage, fully 333km, and the race must finish in time for reports to be in print the next morning. Louis will get by, for today they are approaching country he knows well, passing close by his home. Perhaps here he can make up time—

No. The roads out of Paris are the smoothest of the race so far and the peloton takes advantage, rocketing away up the road. Louis laughs, a gurgling little sound from his tortured lungs, and sets his tempo as the *lanterne rouge.*

Around midday, with a hundred and fifty kilometres on his tyres after twelve hours, he hears the chutter-chutter of an engine approaching on his left. A motor truck comes past, its high sides draped in weatherproof tarpaulin. It passes in front of him but stays to the left and keeps pace, to allow Louis a view of its side.

The tarpaulin is drawn up like a theatre curtain. A lone actor stands on the stage in the tattered uniform and greatcoat of a *poilu,* rifle slung and helmet on. His cheeks are rosied with makeup and his still-life pose is straight from melodrama: a longing middle-distance stare, lips just apart, and a hand over his breast. He waits for his cue.

Louis watches.

Pedal, pedal, pedal.

Nothing happens.

The Actor breaks character. “Amateurs,” he says, nipping to the back of the truck, where Louis now sees a battered gramophone. The Actor sets the needle and returns to his pose.

A song begins, the scratchy audio somehow audible over the noise of the engine. Louis does not know the tune, but it is familiar nonetheless.

Quand il me prend dans ses bras

Il me parle tout bas

Je vois la vie en rose…

“What song is that?” asks Louis.

“It’s not!” snaps the Actor. “Not *yet*, at least. Now quiet, and watch.” He resumes his pose before reaching out toward Louis and addressing an invisible audience. “*Behold, Ellner!* The man of mystery, pedalling so far and so wide, and for what? Many have tried to find out…”

“Only four so far, Monsieur.”

“*Many* have tried to find out, but only one will succeed! *Mesdames et messieurs*, we are proud to present our latest work: *Louis, Le Poilu.*”

A set of cardboard and metal scraps is revealed at the back of the truck-stage. It depicts a trench. The Actor takes a seat on a wooden box and writes a letter in the air.

“Mon amour,” he recites, “I write to you from this terrible place, this place of death and want. Let it end, so I may be in your arms again. I long to ride a tandem with you down the hills of Épernay! I pine for your padded saddle! I ache to grease your spokes!”

Louis giggles. “What does that last line even mean?”

“Shush! Our hero never saw his lost love, but he persevered, and pledged to honour that love by competing in the toughest, most monstrous bicycle race ever staged, and that ever will be staged!” The Actor bows, exhausted by the emotional toll of his performance. “Thank you, thank you.”

“Encore!” shouts Louis.

"*Va te faire foutre*," swears the Actor, "*Et ta maman.* My point is made. It's love that brought you here, Louis. You're competing to honour a passion that flared briefly but oh, *so* brightly!"

"You're wrong, Monsieur. There is no special lady in my life."

"Who said anything about a lady?"

Louis almost crashes his bike. Pain sloshes back into his thighs.

"Aha! Got you!" cries the Actor. "Tricolore won't hear the end of this."

"You have not got me, Monsieur. If I wanted to honour someone, I'd do it with flowers and patisserie, not this. *Mon dieu*, I'm not a madman."

"Of course, you are! Well, I may not have found the right truth, but I've found *a* truth, eh?"

Louis does not answer.

"*Aaaaah!* We Actors always know." He bangs on the back of the cab. "*Allez*, to the next venue! *Bon courage,* Louis! Give the show a good review, eh?"

The truck drives off.

Into the night, with barely a scrap of moonlight to ride by, Louis finally comes to a halt outside a town. It is *the* town, France's fortress heart, a monument to her fallen in all its rack and ruin.

Verdun.

Louis stops, leaning his bike on a concrete bunker. He steps inside, sits, and his eyes begin to droop.

He remembers the fallen.

He remembers friends.

He remembers a lover.

<u>General Classification after Stage 5</u>

1. Deruyter, Charles (Bel)-71hr 24min

21. Ellner, Louis (Fra)-+56hr 16min

Stage #6—Bar-le-Duc-Belfort, 313km

May 9, 1919, 04.00hrs

Louis arrives at the start of Stage 6 in fine condition. He has had a full *sixteen hours* rest between stages. Paradise. He will need it; the Vosges mountains lie ahead, including the feared Ballon d'Alsace. He knows that his gearing won't allow him to pedal 10 km up a seven per cent gradient.

Walking it is, then.

The Saint-Mihiel battlefield which he must first traverse seems almost homely after five similar stages. He presumes now that most of the world is devastated. Trees are meant to be shrapnel-scarred skeletons. Burnt-out trucks are the new civic monuments. The labour battalions are bringing in the harvest of this region's staple crop, barbed wire. They pile it high by the roadside. It is a bumper year.

Hills loom, then mountains. By the time Louis reaches the foot of the Ballon it is almost dark. He begins the walk. The air grows cold, biting at his ankles and his wrists. Up, up, further up, shouldering his bike, pushing it, shouldering it again.

The light is almost gone when he stops dead, puts down his bike, and lets it fall into the snow.

Snow. A metre deep, blanketing the road ahead.

It is an absurd obstacle. The commissaire's cars have not passed through, but the twenty remaining riders have. Louis can see their paths carved through the cold wet wall.

He knows that if he can make it over this, he can walk down the treacherous descent and finish the stage. Stage 7 is much shorter, a gallop for the professionals and achievable for Louis. In other words, if he passes this snow, he will finish the Circuit des Champs de Bataille.

So he walks. He carves a sodden path through the snow, through the dark. He cannot stop. If he stops, he's finished. He knows he should quit. He should have quit on stage three, if not earlier. They might well find his body here in the morning. He should quit.

He sees a light in the woods, spies a house, and quits.

After propping up his bike under the eaves of the timber cabin, he knocks on the door. It opens, revealing a barrel-chested bear of a man and a comely woman in a colourful smock, both in their late middle age and bearing such expressions of welcome that Louis weeps in relief.

"Come in, Louis," says the Wife.

"You've been out in the cold too long," says the Husband.

Louis staggers in, falls on a truckle bed, and is instantly asleep.

It is still dark when he wakes to the smell of meat roasting over pine logs. Louis rises, pulling aside the blanket laid over him. He wears clean vest and trousers. His kit is drying near the fire where the Husband turns a brace of woodcock on a spit. The Wife prepares wooden plates and mugs.

She sees Louis is awake. "Good morning, Monsieur."

"Morning?"

"Just," says the Husband. "It is a new day, only a few hours old."

"Is that supper or breakfast you are cooking?" asks Louis.

"Either." The Husband takes the meat and serves it up at a table of oak so gnarled that it could have been grown, not built. "Come, eat. It is well earned."

Louis, famished, sets to as politely as he can, partaking of bread and steamed vegetables alongside the bird. It fills him more completely than any of the chops and drumsticks that the race provided for competitors. He is tempted to set off for Belfort immediately, but he knows that a guess is coming. Besides, what's another hour or two on his time?

Whilst he eats, though, no question comes. The Husband and the Wife eat beside him. The silence has no awkwardness.

"Thank you both for your kindness," he says after finishing his meal. "You can make your guess now."

"We have no desire to," says the Wife.

"Well..." says the Husband.

"Perhaps *some* desire," says the Wife, "But it can wait. What matters is that you are ready for your road. This mountain is beautiful, but not forgiving."

"Are you its Spirits?" says Louis.

"Of a sort," says the Husband. "We are the Spirit of all France."

"But is that not Madame Tricolore?"

"Ah, Louis. *There* is a question. Tricolore is of France, but not of *our* France. Hers is of ideas and flags and glories. Ours is of hearth and home, river and valley, hill and mountain."

"Her France is France," says the Wife, "But ours is Brittany, Burgundy and Aquitaine, Lille, Marseille and Brest, Francia and Gaul. We are not always in this place and these forms; we are what this land is. We are the old and the new."

"We have brothers in Germany and Spain, sisters in Morocco and Canada, and cousins in Brazil and China," says the Husband. "We quarrel and we fight, but are family still."

"Tricolore has siblings too," says the Wife, sighing. "But she forgets that, and they forget as well."

Louis thinks back to Verdun, St Mihiel, Amiens and the Somme. It is hard to think of any reason for the war, except to win it. "If this is the true France, I am glad of it."

"Not the true France," says the Husband. "That does not exist."

"But we are *a* France," says the Wife. "And we are happy to give you our hospitality."

Louis accepts a last drink of liqueur coffee, its double warmth putting energy in his limbs. The first pale light of dawn creeps in from the window.

"I must go," he says, "Or I will miss the time cut."

"Are they still bothering with that?" says the Husband.

"No. But still."

He puts on his dry kit and shoulders his bags, now packed with fresh food. The Husband and the Wife hold hands to see him away. The Husband rocks back and forth on his toes, glancing at the Wife for approval.

"Fine," she says, rolling her eyes.

"Thank you," says the Husband. "Louis, may I take my guess as to why you entered this race?"

Louis smiles, only a little wearied of it. "Yes, monsieur."

"It is for the love of the land. Not its meaning in songs or poetry, but its pitch and roll, its climbs and descents, its flowers and trees and its sun and rain and wind."

"Monsieur," says Louis, "It is a lovely guess, and I do love those things, but you're even further off than the others."

"Bah!" The Husband stamps his foot in good-natured frustration. "So much for me. *Bon courage,* Louis!"

"*Allez,* Louis," says the Wife. "Be safe and be happy if you can."

The dawn climb to the summit of the Ballon is still fearsome, but the snow seems less cold than the night before. Louis maintains a slow but consistent tramp to the top. When he reaches it, he sees the sun rising in the east.

Belfort is close. It is a beautiful day. He is going to finish the stage, and he is going to finish the race.

General Classification after Stage 6

1. Deruyter, Charles (Bel)-85hr 01min

19. Ellner, Louis (Fra)-+74hr (estimated—arrival time unrecorded)

Stage #7—Belfort-Strasbourg, 163km

May 11, 1919, 10.00hrs

For the professionals May 10th is a day of restless action. The leader Deruyter has a little under two hours on Anseeuw, who has half an hour on Van Lerberghe in third. These are not tremendous margins. One puncture or fall could lose the race. The rest of the top ten will be eager for higher placings or the stage victory.

At the start line, Louis ponders what he has to race for.

Someone else is eager to question him too. Floating above the startline is the familiar figure of Madame Tricolore. She is titanic now, a goddess twenty feet tall, and her red-white-blue train flows behind her for half a mile.

"*Bonne chance*, my boys!" she cries. "One more day, one more sprint in honour of my victory!"

Bang! The nineteen riders are away, eighteen of them straight to a pace far beyond Louis's capability. He feels like a cow chasing a pack of hares. Tricolore follows them, turning her stitched countenance briefly to Louis—"I shall see you at the finish line, Ellner"—and vanishes in a luminous blaze of her colours.

Louis ambles on. After a brief climb near Belfort, it is a mercifully easy stage, almost all downhill. He is still in pain. He can't decide if his lungs and throat feel stripped of their lining or lined with acidic paste. Whatever he eats is good in the mouth and burning in the gullet. He is covered in scabs and bruises. But he will get to the end.

100 kilometres to go. His legs strain on the pedals.

50 kilometres. His saddle sores pain him.

20 kilometres. He begins to smile.

10 kilometres. He begins to laugh.

Five.

Three.

One—*flamme rouge*!

And *done*.

The sun sets over the Strasbourg rooftops. The crowd has left the Place Broglie—Deruyter sprinted to the stage and overall victory about four hours ago—but the commissaires are waiting to shake the hand of the mad *isolé*. They invite him to a nearby hotel for dinner and drinks with the peloton.

"I'll be along soon," he says. "First I have another appointment."

He sits alone with his bike on a street just off the Place. He lies down, his chest heaving, pain flooding him as much as elation.

It is needless pain. He has finished over three entire days down on Deruyter over a mere seven stages. He has come last, earning himself a few hundred francs as the *lanterne rouge*, but once his expenses are taken into account, he has come out with less than fifty in profit.

He didn't need to do this. His exploits over the last two thousand kilometres have been astonishing and senseless.

"So why do you think I did it?" he says aloud. Madame Tricolore stands beside him, reduced to a more relatable size. A Frankish halo encircles her.

"Louis," she says. "I think you've lied to one of us. The Champion, the Hermit, the Giant, the Actor, the Husband and Wife, and I. One of us had the truth, didn't we?"

"Madame, I could not lie to any of you."

"Then tell me!" She comes so close that he can smell her perfume: Provençal flowers, Alpine meadows, the salt of Breton seas and the alcoholic fumes of Montmartre. "If it was not for those things, what for?"

Grimacing with pain, Louis stands up and looks Tricolore dead in her silken eye. "After all this, these two weeks, these five years, do you still think there is one neat reason in my mind? One easy answer to one impossible question? Madame, I rode for all of them. Honour and regret, love and punishment. You and your fellows knew that much of me, it is true. But none of you know me in all, and perhaps I have other reasons besides.

"And here, Madame, is your tragedy. You do not get to know more. The papers will never record my story. I will not keep a diary. History will barely remember me. All you will know is that this was done. I am the *lanterne rouge*, the last man home, and if there is any more to say, no one will know but I.

"Madame, and all of you: *you do not get to know.*"

He wheels his bike away into the Alsatian night.

"Louis?" says Tricolore. "Louis!"

But he is gone.

We will see no more of him.

"*Bonne chance*, Louis," says Madame Tricolore, fading away. A phantasmal tear runs down her fabric cheek. "*Bonne chance.*"

Final General Classification

1. Deruyter, Charles (Bel)-89hr 56min

19. Ellner, Louis (Fra)-+78hr (estimated)

About the Authors

Gwyndyn T. Alexander lives in New Orleans with her husband and cats. She is a poet, artist, and activist.

Gustavo Bondoni is a novelist and short story writer with over three hundred stories published in fifteen countries, in seven languages. His latest novel is *Lost Island Rampage* (2021). Though lacking a permanent beard, he often goes a couple of weeks without shaving, so is often bristly... and you can find him on www.gustavobondoni.com.

C.B. Claywell has a History degree from Murray State University and served in both the Army and Navy for a total of nine years. His degree and many unique experiences gave him a solid background in historical research, writing, and good storytelling, factors that he strives to incorporate into his fiction.

Karl El-Koura lives with his family in Canada's capital city, holds a second-degree black belt in Okinawan Goju Ryu karate, and works a regular job in daylight while writing fiction at night. Visit www.ootersplace.com to learn more about his work.

Rob Francis is an academic and writer based in London. He mainly writes short fantasy and horror, and his stories have appeared in magazines such as The Arcanist, Apparition Lit, Metaphorosis, Love Letters to Poe and Weird Horror. Rob has also contributed stories to several anthologies, including *DeadSteam* by Grimmer & Grimmer books, and *Under* *the Full Moon's Light* by Owl Hollow Press. Rob lurks on Twitter @RAFurbaneco.

David Gerrold is an American science fiction screenwriter and novelist. He wrote the script for the original Star Trek episode "The Trouble with Tribbles", created the Sleestak race on the TV series Land of the Lost, and wrote the novelette "The Martian Child", which won both Hugo and Nebula Awards, and was adapted into a 2007 film starring John Cusack. He has also released Hella, a huge story of colonization set on a huge world.

Bruce Golden's short stories have been published more than 150 times across a score of countries and 30 anthologies. Asimov's Science Fiction described his novel *Evergreen*, "If you can imagine Ursula Le Guin channeling H. Rider Haggard, you'll have the barest conception of this stirring book, which centers around a mysterious artifact and the people in its thrall." His latest book, *Monster Town*, is a satirical send-up of old hard-boiled detective stories featuring movie monsters of the black & white era. It's currently in development for a TV series. http://goldentales.tripod.com.

Yorkshireman **Philip Brian Hall** is a graduate of Oxford University. A former diplomat and teacher, at one time or another he's stood for parliament, sung solos in amateur operettas, rowed at Henley Royal Regatta, completed a 40-mile cross-country walk in under 12 hours and ridden in over one hundred steeplechase horse races. He lives on a very small farm in Scotland. Philip's had short stories published in the USA and Canada as well as the UK. His work has featured in a number of earlier B-Cubed anthologies. His novels, *The Prophets of Baal* and *The Family Demon* are available in e-book and paperback form. He blogs at https://sliabhmannan.blogspot.com/.

James Hancock is a writer/screenwriter who specializes in bizarre comedy, thriller, horror, sci-fi and twisted fairy tales. He takes readers down strange and seldom trodden paths, often dark, and always with a twist or two along the way. He lives in England, with his wife and two daughters. And a bunch of pets he insisted his girls could NOT have.

Liam Hogan is an award winning short story writer, with stories in Best of British Science Fiction and in Best of British Fantasy (NewCon Press). He's been published by Analog, Daily Science Fiction, and Flame Tree Press, among others. He helps host Liars' League London, volunteers at the creative writing charity Ministry of Stories, and lives and avoids work in London. More details at http://happyendingnotguaranteed.blogspot.com/.

Tom Howard is a science fiction and fantasy short story writer living in Little Rock, Arkansas. He thanks his family and friends for their inspiration and the Central Arkansas Speculative Fiction Writers' Group for their perspiration.

Shawn Kobb is an American diplomat by day and writer by night (and sometimes the other way around.) He writes in both novel length and short fiction and focuses on sci-fi, horror, mystery, and fantasy. You can learn more about his writing at https://www.shawnkobb.com/. He currently resides in Budapest, Hungary.

Vlora Konushevci, Albanian poet and literary translator from Kosovo (the newest European state), and lives there with her son, partner and an unused treadmill.

Lita Kurth, MFA- Rainier Writers Workshop, has been published in three genres and nominated for Pushcart Prizes and Best of the Net Awards. Litakurth.com She co-founded a literary reading series in San Jose, The Flash Fiction Forum, and her novel,

The Rosa Luxemburg Socialist Strip Club has been always a bridesmaid, never a bride in numerous contests.

Pedro Iniguez is a speculative fiction writer and painter. His work can be found in publications such as Space and Time Magazine, Crossed Genres, and Tiny Nightmares. Originally from Los Angeles, he now resides in Sioux Falls, South Dakota. He can be found online at https://pedroiniguezauthor.com/.

Al Margrave lives in western Nevada. When he isn't writing short fiction, he often considers writing longer fiction, and has hopes to one day sit at his computer to start.

Alison McBain is a Pushcart Prize-nominated author with work in Flash Fiction Online, On Spec, and Abyss & Apex. Her debut novel, *The Rose Queen*, received the Gold Award for the Literary Classics International Book Awards. *The New Empire*, an alternate history novel to be published in 2022, won the Gold Award for the When Words Count Pitch Contest. When not writing, she's the associate editor for the literary magazine Scribes*MICRO*Fiction.

D. Thomas Minton lives in the mountains of British Columbia. As a tropical marine biologist, he's still trying to figure out how that happened. His fiction has appeared in Asimov's, Lightspeed, Daily Science Fiction, and numerous other magazines and anthologies.

Ann Poore is a poet, harpist, and singer/songwriter, with two CD's to her credit. She lives in Melbourne, Australia, surrounded by her harps and books. She recently retired as a Mental Health Nurse, after many years working with First Responders and Defence Force Personnel with Post Traumatic Stress.

Anthea Sharp is a *USA Today* bestselling author of YA fantasy. Her short stories have been published in collections from DAW books and The Museum of Science Fiction, as well as multiple anthologies. Her newest novel, *Black as Night*, is the second in a trilogy retelling of Snow White and Rose Red featuring hidden magic, an enchanted forest, and two sisters constantly at odds. Find out more at www.antheasharp.com.

Marge Simon is an award-winning poet/writer, living in Ocala, Florida. Her works have appeared in *Daily Science Fiction, Abyss & Apex, New Myths, Silver Blade, Polu Texni, Crannog, JoCCA* and numerous pro anthologies. She is a multiple Stoker winner and Grand Master Poet of the SF & F Poetry Association. She recently received the HWA Lifetime Achievement Award. http://margesimon.com/

Canadian poet, fiction writer, and playwright **J. J. Steinfeld** lives on Prince Edward Island, where he is patiently waiting for Godot's arrival and a phone call from Kafka. While waiting, he has published twenty-two books, including *An Unauthorized Biography of Being* (Stories, Ekstasis Editions, 2016), *Absurdity, Woe Is Me, Glory Be* (Poetry, Guernica Editions, 2017), *A Visit to the Kafka Café* (Poetry, Ekstasis Editions, 2018), *Gregor Samsa Was Never in The Beatles* (Stories, Ekstasis Editions, 2019), *Morning Bafflement and Timeless Puzzlement* (Poetry, Ekstasis Editions, 2020), and *Somewhat Absurd, Somehow Existential* (Poetry, Guernica Editions, 2021).

Peter B. Tacy is a retired educator. He lives in Mystic, CT. Peter and his wife Jane Yolen were pals (and fellow poets) when they were in college in the 1950's. Later both were widowed after long marriages. They re-united in 2019.

Jeremy Thackray writes historical fiction with speculative twists. He's a keen club cyclist, but suspects he's better at writing about bicycles than racing them. If anyone wants to know more about the Circuit de Champs de Bataille, he recommends *Riding* *in the Zone Rouge* by Tom Isitt, which inspired his short story in this collection.**Jim Wright** is a retired US Navy Chief Warrant Officer and freelance writer. He lives in Florida where he watches American politics in a perpetual state of amused disgust. He's been called the Tool of Satan, but he prefers the title: Satan's Designated Driver. He is the mind behind Stonekettle Station (www.stonekettle.com). You can email him at jim@stonekettle.com. You can follow him on Twitter @stonekettle or you can join the boisterous bunch he hosts on Facebook at Facebook/Stonekettle. Remember to bring brownies and mind the white cat, he bites. Hard.

Jane Yolen has published over 400 books and has her eyes on the big 5-0-0. Along the way she's won 2 Nebulas, 3 World Fantasy Awards, The Skylark Award, and a Caldecott Medal for her book OWL MOON. At age 80, she was in a band. She was the first woman to give the Andrew Lang Lecture at the University of St Andrews, Scotland, a lecture series that began in the1920's and included talks by both John Buchan and J.R.R. Tolkien among others. She is a SFWA Grand Master, SFPA Grand Master, and a Grand Master of World Fantasy. At 82, and a widow, she married one of her old college boyfriends.

It has been a great ride with some wonderful people.
I can only hope you all enjoyed this as much as I enjoyed working with Debora and all of these smart writers.

Bob B.

About B-Cubed Press

B Cubed Press is a small press that publishes big books about things that matter.

A percentage of EVERY book we publish is donated to Charity. Usually the ACLU. For this book we made an exception and are donating WIRES.

We can be reached at Kionadad@aol.com.

Our writers gather routinely on the "B Cubed Project Page" on Facebook and we can also be found at BCubedPress.com.

Made in United States
North Haven, CT
18 November 2021